17

Tsutomu Sato

Illustration **Kana Ishida**

Illustration assistants
**Jimmy Stone,
Yasuko Suenaga**

Design **BEE-PEE**

The
Irregular
at
MagicHigh
School

HAYAMA

HAYAMA

HOUSEHOLD STAFF OF THE YOTSUBA FAMILY

HAYAMA — Head Butler
Handles any and all matters.

HANABISHI — Second Butler
Generally responsible for matters requiring the use of force.

KUREBAYASHI — Third Butler
Oversees control facilities.

Above are inner household staff
Below are outer household staff

AOKI — Fourth Butler
Responsible for financial matters.

KURODA — Fifth Butler
Responsible for scouting and deployment of external human resources and management of real estate outside the village.

SHIRAKAWA — Sixth Butler
Hayama's assistant. His wife is the chief maid.

KIMURA — Seventh Butler
Acting village mayor; manages real estate within the village.

OBARA — Eighth Butler
A former traffic cop; manages transit in and out of the village.

The Irregular at Magic High School

The Irregular at Magic High School

MASTER CLANS COUNCIL ARC Ⅰ

17

Tsutomu Sato

Illustration Kana Ishida

YEN ON

NEW YORK

THE IRREGULAR AT MAGIC HIGH SCHOOL
TSUTOMU SATO

Translation by Paul Starr
Cover art by Kana Ishida

MAHOUKA KOUKOU NO RETTOUSEI Vol. 17
©Tsutomu Sato 2015
Edited by Dengeki Bunko
First published in Japan in 2015 by KADOKAWA CORPORATION, Tokyo.
English translation rights arranged with KADOKAWA CORPORATION, Tokyo, through Tuttle-Mori Agency, Inc., Tokyo.

English translation © 2021 by Yen Press, LLC

Yen On
150 West 30th Street, 19th Floor
New York, NY 10001

Visit us at yenpress.com
facebook.com/yenpress
twitter.com/yenpress
yenpress.tumblr.com
instagram.com/yenpress

First Yen On Edition: August 2021

Yen On is an imprint of Yen Press, LLC.
The Yen On name and logo are trademarks of Yen Press, LLC.

Library of Congress Cataloging-in-Publication Data
Names: Satou, Tsutomu. | Ishida, Kana, illustrator.
Title: The irregular at Magic High School / Tsutomu Satou ; Illustrations by Kana Ishida.
Other titles: Mahōka kōkō no rettosei. English
Description: First Yen On edition. | New York, NY : Yen On, 2016–
Identifiers: LCCN 2015042401 | ISBN 9780316348805 (v 1 : pbk.) | ISBN 9780316390293 (v. 2 : pbk.) |
    ISBN 9780316390309 (v. 3 : pbk.) | ISBN 9780316390316 (v. 4 : pbk.) |
    ISBN 9780316390323 (v. 5 : pbk.) | ISBN 9780316390330 (v. 6 : pbk.) |
    ISBN 9781975300074 (v. 7 : pbk.) | ISBN 9781975327125 (v. 8 : pbk.) |
    ISBN 9781975327149 (v. 9 : pbk.) | ISBN 9781975327163 (v. 10 : pbk.) |
    ISBN 9781975327187 (v. 11 : pbk.) | ISBN 9781975327200 (v. 12 : pbk.) |
    ISBN 9781975332327 (v. 13 : pbk.) | ISBN 9781975332471 (v. 14 : pbk.) |
    ISBN 9781975332495 (v. 15 : pbk.) | ISBN 9781975332518 (v. 16 : pbk.) |
    ISBN 9781975332532 (v. 17 : pbk.)
Subjects: CYAC: Brothers and sisters—Fiction. | Magic—Fiction. | High schools—Fiction. |
    Schools—Fiction. | Japan—Fiction. | Science fiction.
Classification: LCC PZ7.1.S265 Ir 2016 | DDC [Fic]—dc23
LC record available at http://lccn.loc.gov/2015042401

ISBNs: 978-1-9753-3253-2 (paperback)
       978-1-9753-3254-9 (ebook)

10 9 8 7 6 5 4 3 2 1

LSC-C

Printed in the United States of America

The Irregular at MagicHigh School

MASTER CLANS COUNCIL ARC ①

An irregular older brother with a certain flaw.
An honor roll younger sister who is perfectly flawless.

When the two siblings enrolled in Magic High School,
a dramatic life unfolded—

Character

Tatsuya Shiba

Class 2-E. Advanced to the newly established magic engineering course. Approaches everything in a detached manner. His sister Miyuki's Guardian.

Miyuki Shiba

Class 2-A. Tatsuya's younger sister; enrolled as the top student last year. Specializes in freezing magic. Dotes on her older brother.

Leonhard Saijou

Class 2-F. Tatsuya's friend. Course 2 student. Specializes in hardening magic. Has a bright personality.

Erika Chiba

Class 2-F. Tatsuya's friend. Course 2 student. A charming troublemaker.

Mizuki Shibata

Class 2-E. In Tatsuya's class again this year. Has pushion radiation sensitivity. Serious and a bit of an airhead.

Mikihiko Yoshida

Class 2-B. This year he became a Course 1 student. From a famous family that uses ancient magic. Has known Erika since they were children.

Honoka Mitsui

Class 2-A. Miyuki's classmate. Specializes in light-wave vibration magic. Impulsive when emotional.

Shizuku Kitayama

Class 2-A. Miyuki's classmate. Specializes in vibration and acceleration magic. Doesn't show emotional ups and downs very much.

Subaru Satomi

Class 2-D. Frequently mistaken for a pretty boy. Cheerful and easy to get along with.

Eimi Akechi

Class 2-B. A quarter-blood. Almost everyone calls her "Amy." Daughter of the notable Goldie family.

Akaha Sakurakouji

Class 2-B. Friends with Subaru and Amy. Wears gothic lolita clothes and loves theme parks.

Shun Morisaki

Class 2-A. Miyuki's classmate. Specializes in CAD quick-draw. Takes great pride in being a Course 1 student.

Hagane Tomitsuka

Class 2-E. A magic martial arts user with the nickname "Range Zero." Uses magic martial arts.

Mayumi Saegusa

An alum. College student at the Magic University. Has a devilish personality but weak when on the defensive.

Azusa Nakajou

A senior. Former student council president. Shy and has trouble expressing herself.

Suzune Ichihara

An alum. College student at the Magic University. Calm, collected, and book smart.

Hanzou Gyoubu-Shoujou Hattori

A senior. Former head of the club committee. Gifted but can be too serious at times.

Mari Watanabe

An alum. Mayumi's good friend. Well-rounded and likes a sporting fight.

Katsuto Juumonji

An alum and former head of the club committee. Has advanced to Magic University. "A boulder-like person," according to Tatsuya.

Koutarou Tatsumi

An alum and former member of the disciplinary committee. Has a heroic and dynamic personality.

Midori Sawaki

A senior. Member of the disciplinary committee. Has a complex about his girlish name.

Isao Sekimoto

An alum and former member of the disciplinary committee. Lost the school election. Committed acts of spying.

Kei Isori

A senior. Former student council treasurer. Excels in magical theory. Engaged to Kanon.

Takeaki Kirihara

A senior. Member of the *kenjutsu* club. Junior High Kanto Kenjutsu Tournament champion.

Kanon Chiyoda

A senior. Former chairwoman of the disciplinary committee. As confrontational as her predecessor, Mari.

Sayaka Mibu

A senior. Member of the kendo club. Placed second in the nation at the girl's junior high kendo tournament.

Takuma Shippou

The head of this year's new students. Course 1. Eldest son of the Shippou, one of the Eighteen, families with excellent magicians.

Kasumi Saegusa

A new student who enrolled at Magic High School this year. Mayumi Saegusa's younger sister.

Minami Sakurai

A new student who enrolled at Magic High School this year. Presents herself as Tatsuya and Miyuki's cousin. A Guardian candidate for Miyuki.

Izumi Saegusa

A new student who enrolled at Magic High School this year. Mayumi Saegusa's younger sister. Kasumi's younger twin sister. Meek and gentle personality.

Kento Sumisu

Class 1-G. A Caucasian boy whose parents are naturalized Japanese citizens from the USNA.

Koharu Hirakawa

An alum and engineer during the Nine School Competition last year. Withdrew from the Thesis Competition.

Chiaki Hirakawa

Class 2-E. Holds enmity toward Tatsuya.

Tomoko Chikura

A senior. Competitor in the women's solo Shields Down, a Nine School Competition event.

Tsugumi Igarashi

An alum.
Former biathlon club president.

Yousuke Igarashi

A junior. Tsugumi's younger brother. Has a somewhat reserved personality.

Kerry Minakami

A senior. Male representative for the main Monolith Code event at the Nine School Competition.

Satomi Asuka

First High nurse. Gentle, calm, and warm. Smile popular among male students.

Kazuo Tsuzura

First High teacher. Main field is magic geometry. Manager of the Thesis Competition team.

Jennifer Smith

A Caucasian naturalized as a Japanese citizen. Instructor for Tatsuya's class and for magic engineering classes.

Haruka Ono

A general counselor of First High. Tends to get bullied but has another side to her personality.

Yakumo Kokonoe

A user of an ancient magic called *ninjutsu*. Tatsuya's martial arts master.

Pixie

A home helper robot belonging to Magic High School. Official name 3H (Humanoid Home Helper: a human-shaped chore-assisting robot) Type P94.

Masaki Ichijou

A junior at Third High.
Participating in the Nine School
Competition this year as well.
Direct heir to the Ichijou family,
one of the Ten Master Clans.

Gouki Ichijou

Masaki's father.
Current head
of the Ichijou, one of
the Ten Master Clans.

Shinkurou Kichijouji

A junior at Third High.
Participating in the Nine
School Competition this
year as well. Also known
as Cardinal George.

Midori Ichijou

Masaki's mother. Warm
and good at cooking.

Akane Ichijou

Eldest daughter of the
Ichijou. Masaki's younger
sister. Enrolled in an elite
private middle school this
year. Likes Shinkurou.

Ushio Kitayama

Shizuku's father. Big shot in the
business world. His business name
is Ushio Kitagata.

Ruri Ichijou

Second daughter of the
Ichijou. Masaki's younger
sister. Stable and does
things her own way.

Benio Kitayama

Shizuku's mother. An A-rank magician who
was once renowned for her vibration magic.

Wataru Kitayama

Shizuku's younger brother.
Sixth grade. Dearly loves his
older sister. Aims to be a
magic engineer.

Ushiyama

Manager of Four Leaves.
Technology's CAD R & D
Section 3. A person
in whom Tatsuya places
his trust.

Harumi Naruse

Shizuku's older cousin. Student at
National Magic University Fourth
Affiliated High School.

Ernst Rosen

A prominent CAD manufacturer.
President of Rosen Magicraft's
Japanese branch.

Toshikazu Chiba

Erika Chiba's oldest brother. Has a career in the Ministry of Police. A playboy at first glance.

Retsu Kudou

Renowned as the strongest magician in the world. Given the honorary title of Sage.

Naotsugu Chiba

Erika Chiba's second-oldest brother. Mari's lover. Possesses full mastery of the Chiba (thousand blades) style of kenjutsu. Nicknamed "Kirin Child of the Chiba."

Makoto Kudou

Son of Retsu Kudou, elder of Japan's magic world, and current head of the Kudou family.

Inagaki

An inspector with the Ministry of Police. Toshikazu Chiba's subordinate.

Minoru Kudou

Makoto's son. Freshman at National Magic University Second Affiliated High School, but hardly attends due to frequent illness. Also Kyouko Fujibayashi's younger brother by a different father.

Anna Rosen Katori

Erika's mother. Half Japanese and half German, was the mistress of Erika's father, the current leader of the Chiba.

Mamoru Kuki

One of the Eighteen Support Clans. Follows the Kudou family. Calls Retsu Kudou "Sensei" out of respect.

Maki Sawamura

An actress who has been nominated for best leading actress by distinguished movie awards. Acknowledged not only for her beauty but also her acting skills.

Harunobu Kazama

Commanding officer of the 101st Brigade's Independent Magic Battalion. Ranked major.

Shigeru Sanada

Executive officer of the 101st Brigade's Independent Magic Battalion. Ranked captain.

Kyouko Fujibayashi

Female officer serving as Kazama's aide. Ranked second lieutenant.

Hiromi Saeki

Brigadier general of the Japan Ground Defense Force's 101st Brigade. Ranked major general. Superior officer to Harunobu Kazama, commanding officer of the Independent Magic Battalion. Due to her appearance, she is also known as the Silver Fox.

Muraji Yanagi

Executive officer of the 101st Brigade's Independent Magic Battalion. Ranked captain.

Kousuke Yamanaka

Executive officer of the 101st Brigade's Independent Magic Battalion. Physician ranked major. First-rate healing magician.

Sakai

Belongs to the Japan Ground Defense Force's general headquarters. Ranked colonel. Seen as staunchly anti–Great Asian Alliance.

Gongjin Zhou

A handsome young man who brought Lu and Chen to Yokohama. A mysterious figure who hangs out in Chinatown.

Xiangshan Chen

Leader of the Great Asian Alliance Army's Special Covert Forces. Has a heartless personality.

Ganghu Lu

The ace magician of the Great Asian Alliance Army's Special Covert Forces. Also known as the "Man-Eating Tiger."

Rin

A girl Morisaki saved. Her full name is Meiling Sun. The new leader of the Hong Kong–based international crime syndicate No-Head Dragon.

Miya Shiba

Tatsuya and Miyuki's actual mother. Deceased. The only magician skilled in mental construction interference magic.

Maya Yotsuba

Tatsuya and Miyuki's aunt. Miya's younger twin sister. The current head of the Yotsuba.

Honami Sakurai

Miya's Guardian. Deceased. Part of the first generation of the Sakura series, engineered magicians with strengthened magical capacity through genetic modification.

Hayama

An elderly butler employed by Maya.

Sayuri Shiba

Tatsuya and Miyuki's stepmother. Dislikes them.

Katsushige Shibata

A candidate to become the next leader of the Yotsuba clan. Employed by the Ministry of Defense. An alum of Fifth High. Specializes in convergence magic.

Yuuka Tsukuba

A candidate to become the next leader of the Yotsuba clan. Twenty-two years old. Former vice president of the First High's student council. Currently a senior attending the Magic University. Strong in mental interference magic.

Kotona Tsutsumi

One of Katsushige Shibata's Guardians. A second-generation Bard series engineered magician. Specializes in sound-based magic.

Kanata Tsutsumi

One of Katsushige Shibata's Guardians. A second-generation Bard series engineered magician. Like his older sister, Kotona, he specializes in sound-based magic.

Angelina Kudou Shields

Commander of the USNA's magician unit, the Stars. Rank is major. Nickname is Lina. Also one of the Thirteen Apostles, strategic magicians.

Virginia Balance

The USNA Joint Chiefs of Staff Information Bureau Internal Inspection Office's first deputy commissioner. Ranked colonel. Came to Japan in order to support Lina.

Silvia Mercury First

A planet-class magician in the USNA's magician unit, the Stars. Rank is warrant officer. Her nickname is Silvie, and Mercury First is her codename. During their mission in Japan, she serves as Major Sirius's aide.

Benjamin Canopus

Number two in the USNA's magician unit, the Stars. Rank is major. Takes command when Major Sirius is absent.

Mikaela Hongou

An agent sent into Japan by the USNA (although her real job is magic scientist for the Department of Defense). Nicknamed Mia.

Claire

Hunter Q—a female soldier in the magician unit Stardust for those who couldn't be Stars. Q refers to the 17th of the pursuit unit.

Rachel

Hunter R—a female soldier in the magician unit Stardust for those who couldn't be Stars. R refers to the 18th of the pursuit unit.

Alfred Fomalhaut

A first-degree star magician in the USNA's magician unit, the Stars. Rank is first lieutenant. Nicknamed Freddie. Currently AWOL.

Charles Sullivan

A satellite-class magician in the USNA's magician unit, the Stars. Called by the codename Deimos Second. Currently AWOL.

Raymond S. Clark

A student at the high school in Berkeley, USNA, that Shizuku studies abroad at. A Caucasian boy who wastes no time making advances on Shizuku. Is secretly one of the Seven Sages.

Gu Jie

One of the Seven Sages. Also known as Gide Hague. A survivor of a Dahanese military's mage unit.

Mitsugu Kuroba

Miya Shiba and Maya Yotsuba's cousin. Father of Ayako and Fumiya.

Ayako Kuroba

Tatsuya and Miyuki's second cousin. Has a younger twin brother named Fumiya. Student at Fourth High.

Fumiya Kuroba

A candidate for next head of the Yotsuba. Tatsuya and Miyuki's second cousin. Has an older twin sister named Ayako. Student at Fourth High.

Kouichi Saegusa

Mayumi's father and the current leader of the Saegusa. Also a top-top-class magician.

Saburou Nakura

A powerful magician employed by the Saegusa family. Mainly serves as Mayumi's personal bodyguard.

Mai Futatsugi

Head of the Futatsugi, one of the Ten Master Clans. Resides in Ashiya, Hyogo Prefecture. Publicly she is the majority shareholder in a variety of industrial chemical- and food-processing companies. Responsible for the Hanshin and Chugoku regions.

Gen Mitsuya

Head of the Mitsuya, one of the Ten Master Clans. Resides in Atsugi, Kanagawa Prefecture. Whether it's public or not is a matter of some question, but in any case, he's an international small arms broker. In charge of the still-operational Lab Three.

Isami Itsuwa

Head of the Itsuwa, one of the Ten Master Clans. Resides in Uwajima, Ehime Prefecture. Publicly the executive and owner of a marine-shipping company. Responsible for the Tokai, Gifu, and Nagano regions.

Atsuko Mutsuzuka

Head of the Mutsuzuka, one of the Ten Master Clans. Resides in Sendai, Miyagi Prefecture. Publicly the owner of a geothermal energy exploration company. Responsible for the Tohoku region.

Raizou Yatsushiro

Head of the Yatsushiro, one of the Ten Master Clans. Resides in Fukuoka Prefecture. Publicly a university lecturer and majority shareholder in several telecommunications companies. Responsible for the Kyushu region, except for Okinawa.

Kazuki Juumonji

Head of the Juumonji, one of the Ten Master Clans. Resides in Tokyo. Publicly the owner of a civil engineering and construction company that primarily serves the armed forces. Shares responsibility for the Kanto region, including Izu, with the Saegusa family.

Glossary

Course 1 student emblem

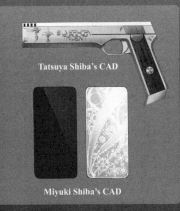

Tatsuya Shiba's CAD

Miyuki Shiba's CAD

Magic High School

Nickname for high schools affiliated with the National Magic University. There are nine schools throughout the nation. Of them, First High through Third High each adopt a system of Course 1 and Course 2 students to split up its two hundred incoming freshmen.

Blooms, Weeds

Slang terms used at First High to display the gap between Course 1 and Course 2 students. Course 1 student uniforms feature an eight-petaled emblem embroidered on the left breast, but Course 2 student uniforms do not.

CAD (Casting Assistant Device)

A device that simplifies magic casting. Magical programming is recorded within. There are many types and forms, some specialized and others multipurpose.

Four Leaves Technology (FLT)

A domestic CAD manufacturer. Originally more famous for magical-product engineering than for developing finished products, the development of the Silver model has made them much more widely known as a maker of CADs.

Taurus Silver

A genius engineer said to have advanced specialized CAD software by a decade in just a single year.

Eidos (individual information bodies)

Originally a term from Greek philosophy. In modern magic, *eidos* refers to the information bodies that accompany events. They form a so-called record of those events existing in the world, and can be considered the footprints of an object's state of being in the universe, be that active or passive. The definition of *magic* in its modern form is that of a technology that alters events by altering the information bodies composing them.

Idea (information body dimension)

Originally a term from Greek philosophy; pronounced "ee-dee-ah." In modern magic, *Idea* refers to the *platform* upon which information bodies are recorded—a spell, object, or energy's *dimension*. Magic is primarily a technology that outputs a magic program (a spell sequence) to affect the Idea (the dimension), which then rewrites the eidos (the individual bodies) recorded there.

Activation Sequence

The blueprints of magic, and the programming that constructs it. Activation sequences are stored in a compressed format in CADs. The magician sends a psionic wave into the CAD, which then expands the data and uses it to convert the activation sequence into a signal. This signal returns to the magician with the unpacked magic program.

Psions (thought particles)

Massless particles belonging to the dimension of spirit phenomena. These information particles record awareness and thought results. Eidos are considered the theoretical basis for modern magic, while activation sequences and magic programs are the technology forming its practical basis. All of these are bodies of information made up of psions.

Pushions (spirit particles)

Massless particles belonging to the dimension of spirit phenomena. Their existence has been confirmed, but their true form and function have yet to be elucidated. In general, magicians are only able to sense energized pushions. The technical term for them is *psycheons*.

Magician

An abbreviation of *magic technician*. *Magic technician* is the term for those with the skills to use magic at a practical level.

Magic program

An information body used to temporarily alter information attached to events. Constructed from psions possessed by the magician. Sometimes shortened to *magigram*.

Magic-calculation region

A mental region that constructs magic programs. The essential core of the talent of magic. Exists within the magician's unconscious regions, and though he or she can normally consciously use the magic-calculation region, they cannot perceive the processing happening within. The magic-calculation region may be called a black box, even for the magician performing the task.

Magic program output process

❶ Transmit an activation sequence to a CAD. This is called "reading in an activation sequence."

❷ Add variables to the activation sequence and send them to the magic-calculation region.

❸ Construct a magic program from the activation sequence and its variables.

❹ Send the constructed magic program along the "route"—between the lowest part of the conscious mind and highest part of the unconscious mind—then send it out the "gate" between conscious and unconscious, to output it onto the Idea.

❺ The magic program outputted onto the Idea interferes with the eidos at designated coordinates and overwrites them.

With a single-type, single-process spell, this five-stage process can be completed in under half a second. This is the bar for practical-level use with magicians.

Magic evaluation standards

The speed with which one constructs psionic information bodies is one's magical throughput, or processing speed. The scale and scope of the information bodies one can construct is one's magical capacity. The strength with which one can overwrite eidos with magic programs is one's influence. These three together are referred to as a person's magical power.

Cardinal Code hypothesis

A school of thought claiming that within the four families and eight types of magic, there exist foundational plus and minus magic programs, for sixteen in all, and that by combining these sixteen, one can construct every possible typed spell.

Typed magic

Any magic belonging to the four families and eight types.

Exotyped magic

A term for spells that control mental phenomena rather than physical ones. Encompasses many fields, from divine magic and spirit magic—which employs spiritual presences—to mind reading, astral form separation, and consciousness control.

Ten Master Clans

The most powerful magician organization in Japan. The ten families are chosen every four years from among twenty-eight: Ichijou, Ichinokura, Isshiki, Futatsugi, Nikaidou, Nihei, Mitsuya, Mikazuki, Yotsuba, Itsuwa, Gotou, Itsumi, Mutsuzuka, Rokkaku, Rokugou, Roppongi, Saegusa, Shippou, Tanabata, Nanase, Yatsushiro, Hassaku, Hachiman, Kudou, Kuki, Kuzumi, Juumonji, and Tooyama.

Numbers

Just like the Ten Master Clans contain a number from one to ten in their surname, well-known families in the Hundred Families use numbers eleven or greater, such as Chiyoda (thousand), Isori (fifty), and Chiba (thousand). The value isn't an indicator of strength, but the fact that it is present in the surname is one measure to broadly judge the capacity of a magic family by their bloodline.

Non-numbers

Also called Extra Numbers, or simply Extras. Magician families who have been stripped of their number. Once, when magicians were weapons and experimental samples, this was a stigma between the success cases, who were given numbers, and the failure cases, who didn't display good enough results.

Various Spells

• Cocytus

Outer magic that freezes the mind. A frozen mind cannot order the flesh to die, so anyone subject to this magic enters a state of mental stasis, causing their body to stop. Partial crystallization of the flesh is sometimes observed because of the interaction between mind and body.

• Rumbling

An old spell that vibrates the ground as a medium for a spirit, an independent information body.

• Program Dispersion

A spell that dismantles a magic program, the main component of a spell, into a group of psionic particles with no meaningful structure. Since magic programs affect the information bodies associated with events, it is necessary for the information structure to be exposed, leaving no way to prevent interference against the magic program itself.

• Program Demolition

A typeless spell that rams a mass of compressed psionic particles directly into an object without going through the Idea, causing it to explode and blow away the psion information bodies recorded in magic, such as activation sequences and magic programs. It may be called magic, but because it is a psionic bullet without any structure as a magic program for altering events, it isn't affected by Information Boost or Area Interference. The pressure of the bullet itself will also repel any Cast Jamming effects. Because it has zero physical effect, no obstacle can block it.

• Mine Origin

A magic that imparts strong vibrations to anything with a connotation of "ground"—such as dirt, crag, sand, or concrete—regardless of material.

• Fissure

A spell that uses spirits, independent information bodies, as a medium to push a line into the ground, creating the appearance of a fissure opening in the earth.

• Dry Blizzard

A spell that gathers carbon dioxide from the air, creates dry-ice particles, then converts the extra heat energy from the freezing process to kinetic energy to launch the dry-ice particles at a high speed.

• Slithering Thunders

In addition to condensing the water vapor from Dry Blizzard's dry-ice evaporation and creating a highly conductive mist with the evaporated carbon dioxide in it, this spell creates static electricity with vibration-type magic and emission-type magic. A combination spell, it also fires an electric attack at an enemy using the carbon gas-filled mist and water droplets as a conductor.

• Niflheim

A vibration- and deceleration-type area-of-effect spell. It chills a large volume of air, then moves it to freeze a wide range. In blunt terms, it creates a super-large refrigerator. The white mist that appears upon activation is the particles of frozen ice and dry ice, but at higher levels, a mist of frozen liquid nitrogen occurs.

• Burst

A dispersion-type spell that vaporizes the liquid inside a target object. When used on a creature, the spell will vaporize bodily fluids and cause the body to rupture. When used on a machine powered by internal combustion, the spell vaporizes the fuel and makes it explode. Fuel cells see the same result, and even if no burnable fuel is on board, there is no machine that does not contain some liquid, such as battery fluid, hydraulic fluid, coolant, or lubricant; once Burst activates, virtually any machine will be destroyed.

• Disheveled Hair

An old spell that, instead of specifying a direction and changing the wind's direction to that, uses air current control to bring about the vague result of "tangling" it, causing currents along the ground that entangle an opponent's feet in the grass. Only usable on plains with grass of a certain height.

Magic Swords

Aside from fighting techniques that use magic itself as a weapon, another method of magical combat involves techniques for using magic to strengthen and control weapons. The majority of these spells combine magic with projectile weapons such as guns and bows, but the art of the sword, known as *kenjutsu*, has developed in Japan as well as a way to link magic with sword techniques. This has led to magic technicians formulating personal-use magic techniques known as magic swords, which can be said to be both modern magic and old magic.

1. High-Frequency Blade

A spell that locally liquefies a solid body and cleaves it by causing a blade to vibrate at a high speed, then propagate the vibration that exceeds the molecular cohesive force of matter it comes in contact with. Used as a set with a spell to prevent the blade from breaking.

2. Pressure Cut

A spell that generates left-right perpendicular repulsive force relative to the angle of a slashing blade edge, causing the blade to force apart any object it touches and thereby cleave it. The size of the repulsive field is less than a millimeter, but it has the strength to interfere with light, so when seen from the front, the blade edge becomes a black line.

3. Douji-Giri (Simultaneous Cut)

An old-magic spell passed down as a secret sword art of the Genji. It is a magic sword technique wherein the user remotely manipulates two blades through a third in their hands in order to have the swords surround an opponent and slash simultaneously. *Douji* is the Japanese pronunciation for both "simultaneous" and "child," so this ambiguity was used to keep the inherited nature of the technique a secret.

4. Zantetsu (Iron Cleaver)

A secret sword art of the Chiba clan. Rather than defining a katana as a hulk of steel and iron, this movement spell defines it as a single concept, then the spell moves the katana along a slashing path set by the magic program. The result is that the katana is defined as a mono-molecular blade, never breaking, bending, or chipping as it slices through any objects in its path.

5. Jinrai Zantetsu (Lightning Iron Cleaver)

An expanded version of Zantetsu that makes use of the Ikazuchi-Maru, a personal-armament device. By defining the katana and its wielder as one collective concept, the spell executes the entire series of actions, from enemy contact to slash, incredibly quickly and with faultless precision.

6. Mountain Tsunami

A secret sword art of the Chiba clan that makes use of the Orochi-Maru, a giant personal weapon six feet long. The user minimizes their own inertia and that of their katana while approaching an enemy at a high speed and, at the moment of impact, adds the neutralized inertia to the blade's inertia and slams the target with it. The longer the approach run, the greater the false inertial mass, reaching a maximum of ten tons.

7. *Usuba Kagerou* (Antlion)

A spell that uses hardening magic to anchor a five-nanometer-thick sheet of woven carbon nanotube to a perfect surface and make it a blade. The blade that *Usuba Kagerou* creates is sharper than any sword or razor, but the spell contains no functions to support moving the blade, demanding technical sword skill and ability from the user.

Magic Technician Development Institutes

Laboratories for the purpose of magician development that the Japanese government established one after another in response to the geopolitical climate, which had become strained prior to World War III in the 2030s. Their objectives were not to develop magic but specifically to develop magicians, researching various methods to give birth to human specimens who were most suitable for areas of magic that were considered important, including, but not limited to, genetic engineering.

Ten magic technician development institutes were established, numbered as such, and even today, five are still in operation.

The details of each institute's research are described below.

Magic Technician Development Institute One

Established in Kanazawa in 2031. Currently shut down.

Its research focus, revolving around close combat, was the development of magic that directly manipulated biological organisms. The vaporization spell Burst is derived from this facility's research. Notably, magic that could control a human body's movements was forbidden as it enabled puppet terrorism (suicide attacks using victims that had been turned into puppets).

Magic Technician Development Institute Two

Established on Awaji Island in 2031. Currently in operation.

Develops opposite magic to that of Lab One: magic that can manipulate inorganic objects, especially absorption-type spells related to oxidation-reduction reactions.

Magic Technician Development Institute Three

Established in Atsugi in 2032. Currently in operation.

With its goal of developing magicians who can react to a variety of situations when operating independently, this facility is the main driver behind the research on multicasting. In particular, it tests the limits of how many spells are possible during simultaneous casting and continual casting and develops magicians who can simultaneously cast multiple spells.

Magic Technician Development Institute Four

Details unknown. Its location is speculated to be near the old prefectural border between Tokyo and Yamanashi. Its establishment is believed to have occurred in 2033. It is assumed to be shut down, but the truth of that matter is unknown. Lab Four is rumored to be the only magic research facility that was established not only with government support but also investment from private sponsors who held strong influence over the nation; it is currently operating without government oversight and being managed directly by those sponsors. Rumors also say that those sponsors actually took over control of the facility before the 2020s.

It is said their goal is to use mental interference magic to strengthen the very wellspring of the talent called magic, which exists in a magician's unconscious—the magic calculation region itself.

Magic Technician Development Institute Five

Established in Uwajima, Shikoku, in 2035. Currently in operation.

Researches magic that can manipulate various forms of matter. Its main focus, fluid control, is not technically difficult, but it has also succeeded in manipulating various solid forms. The fruits of its research include Bahamut, a spell jointly developed with the USNA. Along with the fluid-manipulation spell Abyss, it is known internationally as a magic research facility that developed two strategic-class spells.

Magic Technician Development Institute Six

Established in Sendai in 2035. Currently in operation.

Researches magical heat control. Along with Lab Eight, it gives the impression of being a facility more for basic research than military purposes. However, it is said that they conducted the most genetic manipulation experiments out of all the magic technician development institutes, aside from Lab Four. (Though, of course, the full accounting of Lab Four's situation is not possible.)

Magic Technician Development Institute Seven

Established in Tokyo in 2036. Currently shut down.

Developed magic with an emphasis on anti-group combat. It successfully created colony control magic. Contrary to Lab Six, which was largely a nonmilitary organization, Lab Seven was established as a magician development research facility that could be relied on for assistance in defending the capital in case of an emergency.

Magic Technician Development Institute Eight

Established in Kitakyushu in 2037. Currently in operation.

Researches magical control of gravitational force, electromagnetic force, strong force, and weak force. It is a pure research institute to a greater extent than even Lab Six. However, unlike Lab Six, its relationship to the JDF is steadfast. This is because Lab Eight's research focus can be easily linked to nuclear weapons development, (though they currently avoid such connotations thanks to the JDF's seal of approval).

Magic Technician Development Institute Nine

Established in Nara in 2037. Currently shut down.

This facility tried to solve several problems modern magic struggled with, such as fuzzy spell manipulation, through a fusion of modern and ancient magic, integrating ancient know-how into modern magic.

Magic Technician Development Institute Ten

Established in Tokyo in 2039. Currently shut down.

Like Lab Seven, doubled as capital defense, researching area magic that could create virtual structures in space as a means of defending against high-firepower attacks. It resulted in a myriad of anti-physical barrier spells.

Lab Ten also aimed to raise magic abilities through different means from Lab Four. In precise terms, rather than enhancing the magic calculation region itself, they grappled with developing magicians who responded as needed by temporarily overclocking their magic calculation regions to use powerful magic. Whether their research was successful has not been made public.

Aside from these ten institutes, other laboratories with the goal of developing Elements were operational from the 2010s to the 2020s, but they are currently all shut down. In addition, the JDF possesses a secret research facility directly under the Ground Defense Force's General Headquarters' jurisdiction, established in 2002, which is still carrying on its research. Retsu Kudou underwent enhancement operations at this institution before moving to Lab Nine.

Strategic Magicians: The Thirteen Apostles

Because modern magic was born into a highly technological world, only a few nations were able to develop strong magic for military purposes. As a result, only a handful were able to develop "strategic magic," which rivaled weapons of mass destruction.

However, these nations shared the magic they developed with their allies, and certain magicians of allied nations with high aptitudes for strategic magic came to be known as strategic magicians.

As of April 2095, there are thirteen magicians publicly recognized as strategic magicians by their nations. They are called the Thirteen Apostles and are seen as important factors in the world's military balance. The Thirteen Apostles' nations, names, and strategic spell names are listed below.

USNA

Angie Sirius: Heavy Metal Burst
Elliott Miller: Leviathan
Laurent Barthes: Leviathan
* The only one belonging to the Stars is Angie Sirius. Elliott Miller is stationed at Alaska Base, and Laurent Barthes outside the country at Gibraltar Base, and for the most part, they don't move.

New Soviet Union

Igor Andreivich Bezobrazov: Tuman Bomba
Leonid Kondratenko: Zemlja Armija
* As Kondratenko is of advanced age, he generally stays at the Black Sea Base.

Great Asian Alliance

Yunde Liu: Pilita (Thunderclap Tower)
* Yunde Liu died in the October 31, 2095, battle against Japan.

Indo-Persian Federation

Barat Chandra Khan: Agni Downburst

Japan

Mio Itsuwa: Abyss

Brazil

Miguel Diez: Synchroliner Fusion
* This magic program was named by the USNA.

England

William MacLeod: Ozone Circle

Germany

Karla Schmidt: Ozone Circle
* Ozone Circle is based on a spell codeveloped by nations in the EU before its split as a means to fix the hole in the ozone layer. The magic program was perfected by England and then publicized to the old EU through a convention.

Turkey

Ali Sahin: Bahamut
* This magic program was developed in cooperation with the USNA and Japan, then provided to Turkey by Japan.

Thailand

Somchai Bunnag: Agni Downburst
* This magic program was provided by Indo-Persia.

The International Situation
State of the World in 2096

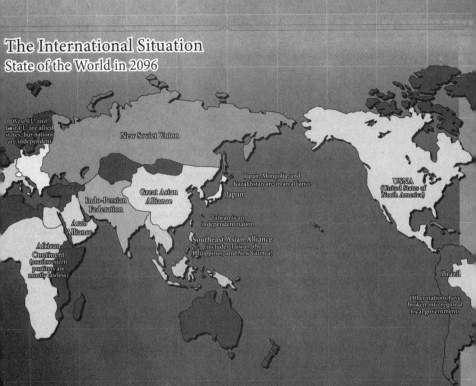

West EU and East EU are allied states, but nations are independent

New Soviet Union

Japan, Mongolia, and Kazakhstan are in an alliance

Japan

USNA (United States of North America)

Indo-Persian Federation

Great Asian Alliance

Arab Alliance

Taiwan is an independent nation

African Continent (southwestern portions are mostly lawless)

Southeast Asian Alliance (includes Taiwan, the Philippines, and New Guinea)

Brazil

Other nations have broken into regional local governments

World War III, also called the Twenty Years' Global War Outbreak, was directly triggered by global cooling, and it fundamentally redrew the world map.

The USA annexed Canada and the countries from Mexico to Panama to form the United States of North America, or the USNA.

Russia reabsorbed Ukraine and Belarus to form the New Soviet Union.

China conquered northern Burma, northern Vietnam, northern Laos, and the Korean Peninsula to form the Great Asian Alliance, or GAA.

India and Iran absorbed several central Asian countries (Turkmenistan, Uzbekistan, Tajikistan, and Afghanistan) and South Asian countries (Pakistan, Nepal, Bhutan, Bangladesh, and Sri Lanka) to form the Indo-Persian Federation.

The other Asian and Arab countries formed regional military alliances to resist the three superpowers: the New Soviet Union, GAA, and the Indo-Persian Federation.

Australia chose national isolation.

The EU failed to unify and split into an eastern and a western section bordered by Germany and France. These east-west groupings also failed to form unions and now are actually weaker than they were before unification.

Africa saw half its nations destroyed altogether, with the surviving ones barely managing to retain urban control.

South America, excluding Brazil, fell into small, isolated states administered on a local government level.

The Irregular at Magic High School

[1]

The notice that came from the Magic Association of Japan on January 2, 2097—right in the middle of the three-day New Year holiday—caused great consternation among the affected parties.

Its author was Maya Yotsuba, head of the Yotsuba family, one of the Ten Master Clans.

It announced the identity of the person who would succeed her as leader of the Yotsuba as well as her heir's betrothal.

This signaled the beginning of the transfer of power to the next generation of Yotsuba leadership. Even to people who didn't recognize the names of Miyuki Shiba, who had been named as Maya's successor, or Tatsuya Shiba, who'd been betrothed to her, the notice carried with it the promise of a new era for Japanese magical society and was immediately received as major news.

But for those who did know Tatsuya and Miyuki Shiba, their shock was over nothing so vague as to what this news might presage for the future but rather something much more concrete and current: Not only were Tatsuya and Miyuki direct descendants (in a sense) of the Yotsuba line, but because their specific relation to the Yotsuba family had been concealed, it was hardly surprising that the revelation came as a true bolt from the blue to all the boys and girls who had variously felt friendship, rivalry, or something greater than that for either of the two.

One such person was Masaki Ichijou, the eldest son of the Ichijou family.

At four o'clock in the afternoon on January 2, Masaki returned from making his New Year's social calls and found himself immediately summoned by his father and so went straight to the Japanese-style sitting room to speak with him.

It was rare for Masaki's father, Gouki, to be home at this hour. Normally, he was either out visiting any number of the work sites for the family's public-facing business, an undersea mining and exploration firm, or overseeing the training of the magicians who served the Ichijou family, and he typically didn't arrive home until dinnertime. But during the three-day New Year's holiday, as the head of one of the Ten Master Clans, he had to be ready to receive callers who would come to deliver their regards for the New Year. Whether he liked it or not was immaterial; it was the duty of the family head to be present in the home.

The Ichijou mansion's private accommodations were built in the Western style, but the public section, meant for receiving guests, had been built in the fashion of traditional Japanese nobility, so reaching the sitting room from the front entrance involved traversing a long hall that wrapped around the building.

Once Masaki arrived at the sitting room where his father waited, rather than immediately opening the sliding shoji door and entering, he took a knee on the wooden floor of the hallway just outside the room.

"I'm here, Father."

"Ah. Well, come on in, then," came the response from the other side of the screen in a rough, world-weary tone.

Masaki, ever youthful and aristocratic, had not inherited his father's demeanor—which was either crude or pleasantly rustic, depending on how one felt—but in either case, he spoke in a distinctively deep, mysterious, and resonant radio voice quality regardless of its volume.

"Excuse me, then," said Masaki as, still kneeling, he slid the partition open, entered, and closed it behind him. Such formality might have seemed excessive between father and son, but the courteous bearing suited Masaki well.

On the other hand, while his father Gouki was wearing a traditional men's kimono and *hakama*, his legs were splayed out roughly and his elbows stuck out well past the armrests at his sides. It was all very reminiscent of the feudal lord style that had been popular in the late Showa era, but Gouki's unrefined aura made it somehow work.

Masaki sat opposite his father. There was not much family resemblance between the two; the sons and daughters of the Ichijou clan were said to favor their mothers, and here, the reputation was undeniably well-earned.

Gouki—forty-two years old this year—was, in a word, manly. His skin was deeply tanned all over, and his short-cropped hair had been bleached brown from long hours in the sun. He had all the dignity that came with his age, but in contrast, his physique bore no trace of decline. His body was well built, though it was the tone of that muscle that was striking, rather than the sheer amount. His facial features, too, were well composed, albeit stern and harsh, and betrayed not a speck of indulgence or mildness.

"You can relax," said Gouki to his son, whose posture had remained faultless.

"In that case, don't mind if I do."

At Gouki's suggestion, his son—who was dressed in his school uniform, which was the appropriate garb for a student making New Year's social calls—stretched his legs out as he released the formal sitting position he'd been in. Gouki was not one for stuffy formality, but there was a line. He was perfectly capable of comporting himself in a manner appropriate to the office when he was acting as the head of the Ichijou family. Masaki understood his father's suggestion to "relax" to mean that he was addressing Masaki not as the head of the Ichijou family but as his father.

"Masaki. When a boy gets to be your age, there are things he might have trouble talking to his father about, but I need you to answer me honestly."

"What's the matter?" It was unusual for the man to preface his statements like this. As one would expect from someone like him, he rarely minced words—particularly not to his own son. Masaki's confusion was understandable.

However, that confusion was about to become profoundly uncomfortable.

"Just answer me honestly. Do you know a girl named Miyuki Shiba?"

"Wh-why would you ask me about that, Father?!"

Masaki's flustered voice alone constituted an affirmative answer, but whether he wasn't perceptive enough to realize that or simply wanted his son to say so explicitly, Gouki pressed the question: "Well, do you?"

Masaki still didn't know why his father was asking, but he did know that this would simply continue until he gave a straight answer, so he nodded resolutely and replied, "...Yes, I do."

"When and where did you come to know her?"

Masaki's initial instinct was to loudly demand why his father was asking. The words got as far as his throat, but just before they were voiced, Masaki realized they would have no effect on their target and corrected course. His father was a blunt man, yes, but he wasn't thoughtlessly rash. There had to be a reason for the question.

"Two years ago at the Nine School Competition. She caught my attention at the preopening party, and I made her acquaintance at the dance held after the closing ceremonies."

"So at first, it was *you* who noticed *her*, then. And if she accepted your invitation to dance, it means she didn't dislike you, at least."

Masaki's face began to burn; he'd provided the barest possible information, but his father had hit the bull's-eye. And yet, these were still the mere opening jabs of the exchange, meant to probe him.

"So you like her, then, this Miss Miyuki?"

Masaki was completely taken aback by his father's mercilessly direct approach. "Wh-what does that have to do with—?"

"I'm asking if you've fallen for the girl."

"And I'm asking you why you would need to know something like that?!" Masaki cried, his tongue finally loosened by embarrassment and frustration.

"About half an hour ago, I received a message from the Yotsuba, via the Magic Association." Gouki met his son's outburst in a grave voice. It had not been his intention to cool the boy's ardor nor poke fun at it.

This was immediately clear to Masaki. His father's tone and the mention of the Yotsuba clan instantly cooled his head. "From the Yotsuba?" he wondered. "What do the Yotsuba want with us?"

"It wasn't directed specifically at our family. It was addressed to the Ten Master Clans, the Eighteen Support Clans, and the Hundred Families. Something of a formality."

"A formality? Don't tell me those stuck-up Yotsubas are suddenly sending everyone well-wishes for the New Year."

Father and son exchanged glances—Masaki to confirm that there was no deception in anything his father was saying and Gouki to see if his son was prepared to accept the truth, regardless of what it might bring.

"It announced that the Yotsuba have selected their next leader—a junior at First High School named Miyuki Shiba."

"Miss Shiba will be…the next head of the Yotsuba…?"

Despite his resolve, Masaki found himself deeply shaken. Miyuki was related to *the* Yotsuba clan? Moreover, she was so closely related that she could be named its next *head*? This rocked him to his core.

Gouki's piercing eyes held his son's gaze. Masaki's racing mind returned to the present in order to hear what his father had to say—but what came next was a still greater blow to the young man's mind:

"Masaki, the Yotsuba have named Miyuki Shiba as their next head. They have also announced her betrothal to her cousin Tatsuya Shiba."

"Miss Shiba is...betrothed...?" he murmured, stunned, before losing his composure entirely. "Cousins? No, Miss Shiba and Tatsuya Shiba are brother and sister!"

Gouki nodded faintly. "That was my understanding as well, and it's true that thus far, they've been presented as siblings. But evidently, the truth is that they are cousins."

Still in the throes of shock, Masaki eventually managed to reply, "*Evidently?*"

"It turns out that Tatsuya Shiba is Maya Yotsuba's son, conceived from an artificially fertilized egg she had cryogenically frozen. They very thoughtfully attached updated family registry data," spat Gouki dubiously. "I have to admit, it's not an implausible story. There's certainly no evidence that would prove any deception on the part of the Yotsuba."

"Do...do you think they're lying, Father?" There was something almost beseeching in Masaki's voice.

"That is not our problem at the moment," barked Gouki, shutting down his son. "Whether they are siblings or cousins, it is still an incestuous betrothal. Our magicians' genetics are a crucial national asset. Any marriage that could damage that genetic legacy is unacceptable. The Ten Master Clans have a clear responsibility to the nation that must be upheld."

Masaki's posture had been deteriorating, but he straightened and composed himself.

"Nonetheless," his father continued, "this is still the Yotsubas' decision to make. The mere possibility of genetic harm isn't enough for us to protest. So again, Masaki, I ask you, do you like Miyuki Shiba? Do you have feelings for her?"

Gouki fixed Masaki with a piercing gaze that would've made even a seasoned sailor flinch. But Masaki had nothing to fear from it. He had no reason to regret his feelings.

"Yes. I do have feelings for her. I fell for her the moment we met."

"Very well." Gouki nodded, satisfied. "In that case, as your father, I would see those feelings answered. There's no need to worry. Akane can lead the Ichijou family. Go marry into the Yotsuba."

"Father?" Masaki was confident that he had truly fallen for Miyuki. He knew his feelings were sincere.

"First, though, you'll have to stop this engagement. Do I need to communicate your intent?"

But he felt very differently about the prospect of his feelings being communicated before he even had a chance to confess them to the girl in question. "Wait a minute, Father!"

"Do you think we have the luxury of time? They've already announced the engagement."

Faced with his father's withering gaze and ruthless logic, Masaki understood that he was outmatched and fell silent.

January 3. In response to the Yotsubas' announcement the previous day to all the numbered families, the Ichijou clan lodged an official protest with the Magic Association of Japan.

This fact was received with intense interest not by the Yotsuba clan itself but rather by Kouichi Saegusa, the leader of the Saegusa family. A faint smile appeared on Kouichi's lips as he scanned the e-paper displaying the protest that Gouki Ichijou had submitted to the Magic Association.

As bold as ever, I see…

Kouichi and Gouki had known each other since they were young men—which was not to say that they were close friends, although neither was there notable animosity between them. Kouichi and Gouki's personalities were merely very different, so they tended to keep what could be most accurately described as a respectful distance from each other.

The gap in their ages was another reason why their relationship lacked much antagonism. By the academic calendar, Kouichi was six years ahead of Gouki. When they'd first met, Kouichi had been a college student, while Gouki was still in middle school. This was why Kouichi had for the most part regarded Gouki as something like a rascally kid brother, which in turn made it difficult to bear him any serious ill will. The protest Gouki had recently lodged was yet another *there he goes again* moment.

If he makes a single misstep, the whole Ichijou family will be caught in the cross fire, though.

The Ten Master Clans all regarded one another as equals, and none held sway over the internal matters of any other. However laudable the cause of safeguarding their genetic legacy might be, no clan had the right to intervene in the affairs of another so brazenly.

However, if one of their clan members *was* personally involved in such a private matter, that was a different story.

In this case, the head of the Ichijou family had not merely opposed the engagement of the successor to the Yotsuba family. In addition to protesting that cousins by mothers who themselves were identical twins were too genetically close to marry, he had also proposed the engagement of the eldest son of the Ichijou family, Masaki, to Miyuki Shiba.

Proposing an engagement to someone who was already betrothed would normally have been a quixotic endeavor. But in this particular case, protecting the valuable genetics of talented magicians was sufficient justification.

Kouichi didn't know whether the Ichijous' true aim was to block the engagement of the future Yotsuba head or simply to support the genuine love of their scion. Personally speaking, Kouichi couldn't imagine making such a gamble for purely sentimental reasons, but he wouldn't put it past Gouki.

Although in this case, it hardly matters.

Kouichi was already quite familiar with both Miyuki Shiba and the boy who'd been named as her intended, Tatsuya.

In addition to mastering high-level magic like Inferno and Niflheim while she was still a freshman at First High, Miyuki Shiba had deployed a completely unknown spell that was instantly lethal during the Yokohama Incident. Whether it was ranged or had an effective radius was still completely uncertain, but the Saegusa family's researchers predicted that as anti-personnel magic, it would be roughly equivalent to Meteor Line.

And then there was Tatsuya Shiba, with his supremely powerful offensive ability, his still mysterious decomposition magic, and his frankly miraculous regeneration magic. Kouichi had received reports that Tatsuya was the strategic-class magician who'd been involved in the Scorching Halloween. And it was plain fact that he had a secret connection to the Defense Force's 101st Brigade's Independent Magic Battalion, who'd successfully deployed flight magic in combat for the first time in history.

Kouichi had known for some time that both of them were directly related to the Yotsuba line. He hadn't known for certain that Tatsuya Shiba was Maya's biological son, but given the lack of definitive proof that Miyuki Shiba was Miya's daughter, he'd had an inkling. Once the two were joined with the Yotsuba around them, not even the united forces of the other Ten Master Clans plus the Eighteen Support Clans would be able to resist them. Kouichi didn't know it, but Retsu Kudou had come to hold the same concern.

The Miyuki Shiba had been designated as the next Yotsuba family head and betrothed to *that* Tatsuya Shiba. Kouichi had been thoroughly rattled upon receiving the news. He had thought that the two were siblings (which, in fact, they were) and had also assumed that Tatsuya would eventually leave the Yotsuba nest. Kouichi hadn't presumed Tatsuya would go so far as to cut all ties with his family, of course, but he'd hoped that with time he'd be able to convince the boy of how important it was to maintain the nation's internal balance of power. Not that Kouichi had any intention of asking how he might actually *do* that convincing, of course.

Thus, Maya revealing the fact that Tatsuya and Miyuki were not siblings but cousins and announcing their sudden engagement was a profound miscalculation on Kouichi's part. The authenticity of her claim that they weren't siblings was beside the point. Nobody was in a position to compel the two to undergo the kind of thorough physical examination that would verify the truth of the matter, so the public statement carried the weight of truth. If the engagement became a marriage, Tatsuya and Miyuki would become the unshakable center of consolidated Yotsuba power, making Kouichi's worst fears a reality.

It already seemed impossible to stop. The news, sent via the Magic Association to all the Numbered families, amounted to a formal engagement announcement. Any opportunity for outside interference was already gone. The fact gnawed at Kouichi. But—

I suppose this is one approach.

Gouki's response wasn't reckless, but it *was* confrontational. Kouichi didn't know how far ahead he'd thought it through, but given Gouki's temperament, it seemed likelier that he hadn't given it much consideration.

But there was no mistaking that it was an *effective* choice.

That was true even now, as Kouichi summoned his daughters to the sitting room.

In contrast to Kouichi in his suit and tie, when his daughters arrived in the sitting room, they were all wearing gorgeous *furisode* formal kimonos. This was not because they wanted to—the three girls had been deliberately dressed this way. Nor was it per their parents' desires. No, such considerations were irrelevant—it was all for the benefit of the guests they were entertaining. In the Saegusa family, it was the eldest son's duty to go out and make the New Year's social calls, whereas the three daughters were entrusted with receiving any callers who arrived. Additionally, Mayumi, Izumi, and Kasumi's mother was staying elsewhere under the pretext of receiving medical care.

"Father, what is it you wanted to see us about?"

The three sisters had scarcely sat down when Mayumi posed the question. She preferred Western-style dresses, and while every year she did manage to pretend pleasant amiability while wearing the stiff kimono, her patience was running thin.

"Yesterday we received two announcements sent from the Yotsuba clan, via the Magic Association, addressed to the Ten Master Clans, the Eighteen Support Clans, and the Hundred Families."

It was Izumi who responded to the bait, and unlike her sister, she seemed untroubled by her garments. She asked precisely the question their father had meant to elicit: "Not just the Twenty-Eight families but the Hundred as well? What could possibly be so important?"

Rather than being sincerely interested, Izumi was clearly just obliging her father, but nevertheless, the man nodded, satisfied. He had always been a bit soft on Izumi, who was his youngest daughter (albeit of twins) and who always seemed to charm the adults around her.

"I'll tell you—and it *is* important. Both for the Yotsuba family and for you all."

"For us, too?" Mayumi wondered.

Kouichi spoke plainly. "The Yotsuba have selected Miyuki Shiba, a junior at First High, as their next family head."

"What?!" Mayumi balked. Izumi's eyes went wide as she clasped her hands over her mouth. Even the relatively more composed Kasumi made a skeptical expression.

Even Mayumi, who'd known the siblings the longest, had

assumed from their surnames that they were members of an extra, non-number family at best, descended from one of the clans associated with the number four. It hadn't crossed any of the three sisters' minds until just this moment that Miyuki might be a member of *the* Yotsuba clan.

"Furthermore, they announced that Miyuki Shiba was engaged to another junior at First High, Tatsuya Shiba."

"No!"

"That's not possible!"

"Surely not even the Yotsuba can have sibling marriages."

Izumi was rendered incoherent, Mayumi cried out in protest, and Kasumi replied with a logical point of order.

"Evidently, they are actually cousins."

"Cousins?" Kasumi prompted. Her composure was not because she was appreciably more coolheaded and calculating than her sisters, but rather because she had little emotional involvement with Tatsuya or Miyuki.

Kouichi was able to grasp this thanks to his good understanding of his daughters' dispositions. He knew that Izumi held Miyuki in particularly high regard—so what piqued his interest now was the reason for Mayumi's intense dismay.

"Miyuki Shiba's mother's maiden name was Miya Yotsuba. Tatsuya Shiba is evidently the biological son of Maya Yotsuba, the current head of the family, conceived from her cryogenically frozen egg."

"Tatsuya is the son...of the family head?" murmured the eldest sister, stunned.

Kasumi gave her a sympathetic look. Her older twin's petrification didn't seem to be weakening anytime soon, so she decided to leave her be. Meanwhile, as he continued, Kouichi's voice took on a sharper edge, and Kasumi gave him her full attention.

"In reaction to this, Gouki Ichijou, the head of the Ichijou clan, sent a protest via the Magic Association, demanding that Miyuki and Tatsuya's engagement be dissolved."

"The Ichijou clan?" asked Mayumi, confused.

"Correct. But since they'd have no right to protest if a personal distaste was all they had, Gouki also proposed to Maya Yotsuba that his oldest son, Masaki, should be engaged to Miyuki."

"I see…"

Mayumi had recovered from her dismay and was now considering the possible implications and motives behind the potential engagement of the Ichijou scion to the next Yotsuba family head.

"Do you have any insight, Mayumi?" The girl's shock had faded, which her father appreciated. She was always quick to adapt.

"No, nothing really significant. Only that I remember Masaki Ichijou having a rather strong affinity for Miyuki."

"Tell me more. When did you notice it?"

"At the after-party for the Nine School Competition before last. I doubt I was the only one who noticed."

Mayumi's information was surprisingly useful. Apparently, the Ichijou head's motivation was primarily to support the romantic aspirations of his son. "I see. So Ichijou's actions weren't political but rather out of consideration for his son's feelings."

Kouichi knew he could never think the way Gouki did. He'd never compromise the Saegusa family's position just to help his daughters in love—but at the same time, he could see why Gouki's principles would be better received by his daughters than his own would be.

"Incidentally, girls, what kind of boy would you say this Tatsuya Shiba is? What's your opinion, Mayumi?"

His question brought a degree of turmoil back to Mayumi's eyes. "I mean…he's a very talented underclassman."

Despite this noncommittal answer, Kouichi hardly failed to notice the faint flush that colored his daughter's cheeks. "What about you, Kasumi?"

"I haven't had many chances to interact with him personally, so all I can tell you is that he's very knowledgeable and extremely skilled with magic engineering," she replied, her expression remaining composed as she glanced at her twin sister who had not yet spoken on the subject. "Izumi works with him on the student council, so she would know more than I do."

"I see." Kouichi turned to Izumi. "What do you make of him, then?"

Izumi, caught with a vacant expression on her face, came to her senses at the sound of her name. She made no pretense of trying to give a calm answer; instead, her expression tightened. "...He is...a person who's impossible to evaluate for someone like me."

"Huh."

It wasn't only Kouichi whose face betrayed surprise. Kasumi gazed openly at his daughter in interest, while Mayumi turned her whole body toward Izumi, her eyes wide.

Unperturbed, Izumi straightened herself, and, looking her father square in the eyes, continued. "Father, I believe you're aware of the stellar furnace experiment that was held at First High last March, right?"

"Yes—now that you mention it, Tatsuya Shiba played a key part in that, didn't he?" The incident had upset Kouichi's scheme to damage the Yotsubas' public reputation. How could he forget?

"After that, Tatsuya performed brilliantly as one of the technology staffers at the Nine School Competition. I've also heard that he was the one who introduced the use of flight magic into the Mirage Bat event, even though flight magic had only just been unveiled at the previous year's competition."

Kouichi also knew this, but he turned to Mayumi for confirmation.

"It's true. He achieved flight magic using competition-specified CAD. He's also developed new magic programs that have been recognized and recorded in the National Magic University's encyclopedia."

"This year he's been asked by competitors to help develop improved versions of high-level magic like Invisible Bullet and Phonon Maser," Izumi added, following Mayumi's confirmation.

"That's very impressive." Kouichi already knew everything his daughters were telling him, but he affected an easy surprise, as if this were all new to him.

But Izumi had more to say: "The reason I feel that he's impossible to estimate is that it never seems like he considers his achievements to be particularly impressive. Tatsuya...sees things on a fundamentally different level compared to the rest of us. Even when he's standing in the same place, he's living in a different world. That's how it seems to me sometimes."

"Do you mean that he has special vision ability, like Mayumi?"

"...I don't know. This is all just based on my intuition and not much else. I'm...sorry, Father." Izumi looked down sadly, unable to better articulate what she was feeling.

Kouichi looked to Mayumi, who shook her head, indicating that she had no insight to offer, either.

Izumi's impression of Tatsuya had sparked Kouichi's interest, but there wasn't enough information to draw any conclusions, so he set aside his curiosity for the moment. "Well, what do you think of him romantically, then?"

Startled, Izumi looked up and shook her head rapidly, her eyes wide in surprise. "He's totally out of my league! ...Unfortunately. *Very* unfortunately."

Izumi's suddenly resentful muttering was so out of character for her that Kouichi was more disturbed than he was worried. "Izumi, what happened?"

"If only I were desirable enough to catch Tatsuya's eye...! Then I wouldn't have to stand by and watch as Miyuki is—"

"Izumi, do you have any idea what you're saying? Honestly, you're freaking *me* out a little here!" interjected Kasumi, who was shocked enough by Izumi's odd behavior to let her formality slip in front of her father.

Kouichi cleared his throat awkwardly.

Kasumi and Izumi flinched and together corrected their posture and looked down shamefacedly.

Kouichi didn't scold either of them further—he was hesitant to give them any more stimulation of any kind—and instead turned to Mayumi. "Mayumi, what about you? What do you make of Tatsuya Shiba as a romantic partner?"

"What do I make of him? I mean…" Mayumi cast her gaze around uncertainly, despite having suspected a question like this would be coming. She didn't seem to hate the prospect, at least.

"Tatsuya is two years younger than you, but that's not such a terrible age gap. And as the son of the current head of the Yotsuba, his social standing's certainly adequate," said Kouichi.

"It's very hard for me to think of him as younger than me, yes, but…"

If anything, he was *more* suitable than any of the prospects Kouichi had considered for Mayumi thus far. This might actually work. If he coordinated with Gouki, they might actually be able to foil Maya's scheme.

"Well, Mayumi, if that's how you feel, then we should formally contact the Yotsuba clan and—" Kouichi began, only to be interrupted by Kasumi.

"I'm opposed!"

"Kasumi, restrain yourself," he scolded his impertinent daughter immediately, not just because she'd interrupted him but because she was old enough to know better.

"…I apologize, Father," Kasumi said, shamed. She still seemed displeased but did not argue the point.

"Father, while I agree that there's nothing wrong with Mayumi pursuing Tatsuya in principle, I am also opposed to this."

Having just taken a firm hand with Kasumi, Kouichi appeared willing to listen to what Izumi had to say. She'd been more polite, which was part of it, but Kouichi was also—as ever—prone to dote on her. "And why is that, Izumi?"

"It would be scandalous for a woman to approach a man whose engagement has already been announced. The Ichijou clan's plan only works because Masaki is a man. Tatsuya's also a man, so it's easy for him to laugh off an attempt to interfere—but in the opposite case, Miyuki would certainly take offense."

"…Is that how it works?" Once it had been pointed out, even Kouichi couldn't dismiss the emotions of the women involved.

"Yes, it is!" answered Mayumi, taking advantage of the moment. "Proposing a relationship with a man who's just announced his engagement would ruin my reputation! And worse, I'm older than him—people would say I'm a scheming villainess trying to seduce a younger man. No *thank* you."

"Ah, I see."

Right there on the spot, Kouichi abandoned any attempt to interfere with the engagement that the Yotsuba family had announced. He cautioned his daughters to remember henceforth that whenever they interacted with Tatsuya or Miyuki to bear in mind that they were direct blood relatives of the Yotsuba line and then dismissed the girls.

By eight o'clock in the evening, the last of the New Year's guests had left the Saegusa home. There were no banquet plans until the next day, so after eating dinner with his daughters—who'd changed out of their formal kimonos—Kouichi retired to his study.

It was not terribly different from the way he spent his time on any other day. He didn't often take meals with his daughters, but after dinner he always spent time in his study. As he skimmed the correspondence pertaining to his work as the head of one of the Ten Master Clans, his work managing his public-facing business, and the work that had to be kept secret, his mobile phone rang.

"Mr. Saegusa, many happy returns on the New Year."

The caller was Gouki Ichijou.

"Mr. Ichijou, Happy New Year to you. It's very kind of you to call."

"No, I'm sorry to have kept you waiting."

"I haven't been waiting too terribly long."

About two hours earlier, Kouichi had sent Gouki a text asking him to call when he had a chance. Whether Kouichi's reassurance that he hadn't been kept waiting long was the truth or mere social nicety was unclear.

"So I assume you want to talk about what's going on with the Yotsuba?"

There was seven years between the men, with Kouichi being the older of the two. Despite that, Gouki had started the conversation speaking in an informal register. It was something of an unwritten rule that formality was not necessary among heads of the Ten Master Clans, though, so Kouichi would've found more formality to be inappropriate.

Just because they were polite didn't mean nobody among the Ten Master Clans would ever nitpick trivialities, however.

"That's right. More precisely, I want to talk about the proposal you made to the Yotsuba regarding your son," Kouichi began, a faint smile on his face.

On the screen, Gouki's responded with a scowl.

"Don't leap to any conclusions, please," Kouichi rushed to assure, having anticipated Gouki's reaction. "My only intention is to support your son in his romantic pursuit."

"Oh, is that so? Well, thank you," Gouki offered, expression still wary.

"I find the engagement that Ms. Yotsuba announced to be utterly appalling."

Gouki's expression shifted from suspicion to acceptance. This he could easily understand. *"So I take it that you also think the engagement the Yotsuba clan has announced is a dangerous one?"*

"I do. I've often heard from my daughters about how exceptional Miyuki Shiba is."

This was a lie. Kouichi did not speak to his daughters frequently enough to "often" hear anything. What information he had about Miyuki and Tatsuya Shiba he had collected mostly independently.

But if Kouichi admitted to that, it would raise the question of why he'd investigated them before their Yotsuba heritage had been made public. Gouki wouldn't understand the answer anyway, so it was much more convenient to simply say he'd heard about Miyuki from his daughters.

"We can't turn a blind eye to the possibility of such profound talent being diminished by not being passed on to her children."

Kouichi's statement was meant to flatter Gouki's position, but Gouki's face surprisingly darkened in a scowl, his lip curling. *"This isn't only about Miyuki. Tatsuya is the magician who beat my son. Call me a doting father if you will, but beating Masaki makes Tatsuya quite a prize himself."*

"It does. You're absolutely right," Kouichi said, immediately admitting his mistake. Whether Gouki was too proud of his son or not, there was unmistakable value in having beaten Masaki Ichijou in magical feats. In fact, when the Third High team captained by Masaki lost to the First High team led by Tatsuya, it had been such an upset that the Magic Association had convened a special online meeting of the Master Clans Council using their dedicated telecommunications line. "Tatsuya Shiba's talent must also be properly valued."

Kouichi's immediate agreement with Gouki's point wasn't just talk.

"So what do you plan to do about it, Mr. Saegusa? Are you saying you'll petition Ms. Yotsuba to dissolve the engagement and support my son?"

Gouki used the word *support*, but he couldn't hide the suspicion on his face—it was obvious that he suspected Kouichi of intending to use his son for his own gains.

Kouichi decided to play the card he'd been hiding: "In fact, I had been thinking of having Mayumi marry Tatsuya and taking him as my son-in-law."

Just as he'd hoped, Gouki was immediately agitated, unable to hide his surprise.

"...*Wasn't Mayumi seeing a boy from the Itsuwa family?*"

Seeing that, Kouichi pressed forward. "Yes, well, it seems neither my daughter nor Hirofumi Itsuwa are terribly interested. I'm not really seeing much willingness to pursue the relationship from either of them, so I've been thinking it's back to the drawing board."

"*And your Mayumi—she's interested in Tatsuya?*"

"Tatsuya was an underclassman of hers, but she doesn't seem opposed to the idea—that's for certain. She'll turn twenty this year, and as her father, I'd certainly like to see her married soon."

Gouki had intuitively grasped that Kouichi was attempting to use the Ichijou family, but his understanding wasn't deep enough to prove it. There wasn't anything amiss in what Kouichi was saying, and Gouki needed all the allies he could get.

"I'm embarrassed to admit that I'm still trying to convince her, though. We haven't gotten to the point where I can send a formal proposal to the Yotsuba clan. In lieu of that, I'd like to add my name in support of your objection."

Gouki felt as though the jaws of a clever trap were closing on him, but he had no choice but to accept the offer. "*Our family would certainly be grateful for your support.*"

"And I'm grateful to have the opportunity to give it. I'm considering contacting others who might be harmed by Ms. Yotsuba's decision—what do you think?"

"*If there are any, by all means, please introduce them to me.*" Gouki was trying mightily to protect his own agency instead of giving Kouichi carte blanche to act as he pleased.

"Yes, of course," said Kouichi with a smile.

The expression as it was displayed on Gouki's screen was as unreadable as ever, and Gouki gave up trying to discern the truth. "*In that case, I'll send you the original letter I submitted to the Magic Association later.*"

"I'll return a cosigned version to you for your confirmation."

"Understood."

"All right. Thank you, Mr. Ichijou."

"Not at all. Thank you. Good-bye."

Thus, the telephone conversation with Gouki concluded very much to Kouichi's satisfaction.

On Friday, January 4, Tatsuya and Miyuki were escorted to their residence by Minami.

Only the top echelon of the magic world had been informed of Tatsuya and Miyuki's connection to the Yotsuba, but it would not take long for the information to spread much more widely. Their residence was still a secret for now, but that, too, would only last so long. They'd been informed that Hayama was preparing the Yotsubas' Tokyo residence for them, and they would probably have to consider moving there in the near future.

But even if they did, Tatsuya estimated they had a month or two before it happened. There were other things to take care of first.

In the previous century, in order to properly receive and entertain guests during the New Year, households had to do a deep, thorough cleaning. Modern homes, though, had largely automated domestic chores, and the cleaning was mechanically managed. After having lunch at home, Tatsuya and Miyuki left Minami there and headed for Yakumo's temple, Kyuuchouji.

Tatsuya again wore a suit and tie, but Miyuki donned a colorful formal kimono with distinctly long sleeves. Taking Tatsuya's motorcycle wasn't a good option, and roller skates were out of the question. Fortunately, both Tatsuya's residence and Kyuuchouji were within the range of the public traffic control system, so they used the residence's self-driving car.

It took about fifteen minutes to arrive at Kyuuchouji. Just before departing, they'd called ahead to confirm their plans, so there was no need to worry whether anyone would be home when they arrived.

However, upon arriving, Tatsuya and Miyuki were still forced to wait for some time. Yakumo was there, yes, but he was seeing other guests. Those guests had arrived just before Tatsuya and Miyuki, *and* without making arrangements ahead of time, but they were apparently the sort of guests who couldn't be turned away—or so one of Yakumo's familiar top disciples explained deeply apologetically.

Tatsuya considered leaving and coming again later, but the disciple eventually convinced him to stay and wait. There weren't any other pressing plans for the day, and Tatsuya didn't really feel like working, so he ultimately decided he didn't mind too much.

It was about half an hour before Tatsuya and Miyuki were summoned into the temple.

As they made for the main hall from the temple residence, they emerged into the garden, whereupon Tatsuya saw the receding form of the previous guest.

It was an old man, his head shaved like a monk's. At first, Tatsuya made him out to be a functionary from the temple's Buddhist sect but quickly realized otherwise. His head was bald, yes, but he was wearing a tailored suit and coat. Sure, some Buddhist clergy wore suits, but Tatsuya got the feeling this wasn't one of them. At the very least, he gave off the strong impression of someone whose power was quite secular.

Sensing Tatsuya's gaze, the old man looked back over his left shoulder.

His left eye was clouded white.

The gesture made Tatsuya deeply uneasy. If there was really a problem with his left eye, then he ought to have looked over his right shoulder, which meant...

That clouded left eye of his saw with something other than mere normal vision.

The old man soon turned away and continued out of the temple gate.

"Tatsuya?"

At the sound of Miyuki's voice, Tatsuya returned to himself with a sharp intake of breath—the old man had thoroughly distracted him.

Unsure of what it was that he was so afraid of, Tatsuya collected himself.

As he knelt in front of Yakumo, Tatsuya didn't ask the identity of the old man he'd spotted in the garden. "My apologies for the late greeting, master. Happy New Year."

Tatsuya didn't feel it was appropriate to demand information about other people's guests. And although he didn't know why, he had the feeling that even if he did ask, his question wouldn't be answered.

Alongside Tatsuya, Miyuki bowed politely.

"Happy New Year. I understand your situation, so you needn't worry," said Yakumo.

Hearing this, the siblings looked up.

"Oh, so you know? I guess I shouldn't be surprised," Miyuki said with an admiring look in her eyes.

Yakumo laughed and shook his head. "No, no. It's nothing to be impressed by. The news about your new title and engagement has traveled quite widely, you see."

"…It's already gone so far?" Tatsuya asked bitterly.

Yakumo widened his eyes in surprise at the question. "Why, of course it has. This is major news in the magic world. A peek inside the inner workings of the mysterious Yotsuba clan! No wonder it's got people's attention. And with the Master Clans Council coming up so soon, too. And this year's assembly is the one that will determine the makeup of the Ten Master Clans for the next four years—big news arriving right before that is bound to travel quickly."

Tatsuya frowned, and Miyuki's expression clouded over. Though the announcement had been limited to the Twenty-Eight Families and the Hundred, they'd known that once it passed through the Magic Association it would spread widely. It had been, after all, a measure to make third parties acknowledge Tatsuya and Miyuki's existence. Putting their names on the lips of everyone in the world of magic had been the Yotsuba clan's plan all along.

But that was merely what Maya wanted, not anything Tatsuya or Miyuki wished for. Setting aside what the rest of the world might think, they were both depressed at the thought of the reception that might be waiting for them when they returned to school.

"Still…to think that you're not siblings but cousins and engaged to boot." Yakumo grinned. "I must admit I never saw this coming. Congratulations."

Miyuki blushed and looked aside at Yakumo's well-wishes. But what he said next made her stiffen.

"So—how much of it is true?" asked Yakumo with a meaningful grin.

Tatsuya's eyes were half-lidded and his expression blank. "We've been told that it is true," he said without much conviction.

"Ah, you've been *told*, eh?"

"With no memory of the events in question, I have little choice but to trust what other people tell us."

Yakumo smiled even as he fixed Tatsuya with a cold gaze. "Ah yes, I see—I see. Not even the great Tatsuya remembers the moments after his own birth, I suppose. And of course, no one can be expected to have direct knowledge of events that occurred before their birth. That stands to reason."

All Tatsuya could do was look downward, his agreement implicit.

After twenty or so minutes more of lively and (only) idle chatter, Tatsuya and Miyuki stood.

Yakumo likewise stood and followed them as they left. Both Tatsuya and Miyuki knew that no matter how much they might try to ask that he not go to the trouble, Yakumo would find their insistence meaningless. Sandwiched between the disciple tasked with escorting them out on one side and Yakumo on the other, they passed through the gate leading to the temple's parking area.

Tatsuya and Miyuki turned to give their regards to Yakumo one last time, but he beat them to the punch.

"Now then, Tatsuya—tomorrow's training is going to be rough, so be ready for it."

Tatsuya's eyes widened. Yakumo's words implied that he needn't worry about any of this and that his training could advance normally. The man was making it clear that their relationship would continue the same as always, regardless of Tatsuya's now-public status as a member of the Yotsuba family.

Tatsuya, of course, did not betray his surprise. "I look forward to another year of training with you, master."

"And master—thank you so much," Miyuki added, her eyes just slightly misty.

The day after paying their respects at Kyuuchouji, Tatsuya left Miyuki at home and paid a visit to the National Defense Force 101st Brigade's base.

His destination was the headquarters of the Independent Magic Battalion—not for training, but to visit Kazama and the rest of the unit.

Tatsuya wore civilian clothes (a suit), but his ID card gave him the same privileges as any officer. He breezed through the gate after passing the card reader and bio-scanner, proceeding on foot to the building that served as the battalion's HQ. He had planned to see Kazama immediately, but in the lobby of the hardened building with its three aboveground and three underground floors, he caught sight of another familiar face.

"Happy New Year, Specialist Ooguro."

"And to you, *First Lieutenant* Fujibayashi. And congratulations."

Tatsuya and Fujibayashi exchanged their New Year's salutations, with Tatsuya adding his congratulations.

"Thank you, Specialist. I certainly am happy with the salary bump," Fujibayashi quipped.

Tatsuya had the feeling that there was a more complex sentiment hidden beneath her joking answer, but this wasn't the place to ask about it. "I'd like to give my regards to the lieutenant colonel as well," he said.

"Of course. The commander's waiting for us. Come on, then," Fujibayashi said with a pleasant smile, turning on her heel.

Tatsuya followed dutifully behind.

It seemed there was only one person in the commander's office, so Fujibayashi knocked at the door. "It's Fujibayashi, sir."

Kazama answered with permission to enter: "Come in."

"Sir. I've brought Specialist Ooguro with me."

"Both of you, have a seat and wait a moment, would you?" the lieutenant colonel said as he activated something at the console on his desk. A section of the wall opposite the office's entrance tilted down until it was horizontal, becoming a seating surface.

Tatsuya and Fujibayashi sat on the impromptu bench. It was cushioned and not at all uncomfortable.

The computer display on Kazama's desk was tilted back about fifteen degrees; he glanced at it and signed several documents in rapid succession with a stylus before looking at his visitors.

Fujibayashi and Tatsuya got to their feet and approached the desk as Kazama stowed the display within it.

Tatsuya moved a half step ahead of Fujibayashi and saluted. "My regards for the New Year, Commander. And congratulations on your promotion."

Kazama's expression softened, and he stood. "Mm-hmm. Thank you."

The floor behind Fujibayashi and Tatsuya opened up, revealing two sofas that emerged from the gap and inflated.

"For starters, why don't you have a seat?" suggested Kazama as he himself settled down on the simple air-cushioned couch.

Tatsuya sat opposite him on the couch nearest the office's door.

Above them, a ceiling panel lowered to become a suspended table between the couches, on which a tea set including a hot water pitcher, a teapot, and teacups waited.

Still standing, Fujibayashi took the pitcher and poured hot water into the teapot, then after a moment served the freshly brewed tea into the two waiting teacups and set them in front of Tatsuya and Kazama. She smiled at Tatsuya's thanks, then moved to stand beside Kazama.

"Now then, I don't think you have any pressing matters for us, but did you really come all this way just to say *Happy New Year?*" Kazama asked as he reached for his teacup. Although its contents weren't scalding, the pale celadon teacup ought to have been fairly hot to the touch nonetheless, but Kazama betrayed no such sensation.

Tatsuya answered Kazama's candid question with a smile. "I could hardly ignore news of your promotion, Commander." It was a polite smile, but that didn't mean the sentiment behind it was insincere. He'd simply chosen it over a more serious expression.

"My promotion, huh?" Kazama met Tatsuya's smile with his own—but it was a rueful one. "My pay hardly went up, and I'm one of the last of my cohort to get the nod. But if my rank going up makes it easier for my subordinates to stay out of sticky situations, I'm glad for that, at least."

Just as Kazama alluded, his hadn't been the only promotion that was announced that January 1. As Tatsuya had implied earlier, Fujibayashi had gone from second lieutenant to first lieutenant, while Sanada and Yanagi had been similarly promoted from captain to major.

An operation Kazama had been involved in early in his career had incurred the disfavor of the central government, and it had adversely affected his advancement, despite his performance, ability, and reputation. Once he became the commanding officer of the Independent Magic Battalion, the efforts of Major General Saeki—the 101st Brigade's commander—helped him reach colonel, but the bureaucrats at the top of the military had no intentions of letting him advance any further.

But his actions in the Yokohama Incident could not be ignored. With the pretense that the Independent Magic Battalion was a secret unit and therefore immediately awarding them with higher rank would expose them, the promotions had been postponed from the previous January to July, but the voices demanding that meritorious service be properly recognized could no longer be suppressed, so a few days earlier, the announcement of his rise to lieutenant colonel went out.

And along with that came the delayed promotions of Sanada, Yanagi, and Fujibayashi.

"It's not a bad thing to be promoted. Even a small salary increase is never unwelcome," Tatsuya replied.

"Well, that's true. Although my feelings about your income are a bit more complicated."

"It's not as though my income is an order of different magnitude. The market for CADs and other products in the magic engineering field is rather small, after all."

Tatsuya and Kazama shared a chuckle and a grimace.

"Colonel," Tatsuya went on, "how capable is your counterespionage?"

"More than adequate." Kazama nodded.

Tatsuya took a short breath. "Have there been any recent changes to the composition of the battalion?"

"Not at this time. My battalion is classified as a special unit, so the brigade commander doesn't consider it a problem if ranks and roles don't exactly match up perfectly."

"Understood."

Tatsuya had been attached to the Independent Magic Battalion as a special officer, but his position was highly contingent on his personal connections to Kazama and Sanada. If there was a change in upper management, Tatsuya would need to change how he approached his role.

He very sincerely felt the need to weigh any possible impact—positive or negative—to the Yotsuba family. If he were placed under the command of someone he couldn't personally trust, he would have to consider cutting ties with the military. For the moment, at least, that didn't seem too likely.

Next, it was Kazama who put a question to Tatsuya, in a rather stiff tone. "Can we continue to count on your support, Tatsuya?"

"Yes, sir," Tatsuya answered.

"You haven't been given new responsibilities by the Yotsuba clan?"

"Nothing that will conflict with the interests of the Independent Magic Battalion, no." Tatsuya had very deliberately said *the battalion* rather than *the military*. "At least, not at present."

"I see." The meaning of that final qualifier was not lost on Kazama. He paused for a moment before continuing. "In recent months, the global situation has been destabilizing, domestic affairs included. Wars haven't started breaking out again yet, but it's our belief that the likelihood of a medium-intensity conflict sparking in the East Asian region has become quite high. And we expect one soon—specifically, within the next year."

"By *we*, do you mean the army staff or the joint staff?"

Immediately following the Twenty Years' War, Japan's defense forces had been drastically reconceived. The Joint General Staff was folded into the Ministry of Defense, unifying National Ground Defense Force Command, National Maritime Defense Force Command, and National Air Defense Force Command. A General Staff Council was established as a temporary agency attached directly to the Joint General Staff, with the chairman of the Joint Staff acting as its head. And in times of emergency, the General Staff Council could be convened to act as the defense force's highest decision-making body.

As an example, during the Yokohama Incident, within two hours after the outbreak of hostilities, the General Staff Council convened and authorized the deployment of Material Burst.

Under the current regime, the general headquarters of the army, navy, and air forces each had a staff section responsible for intelligence processing and operational planning, but separate from those, the Joint Staff also had a cross-organizational department that provided intelligence analysis and perspective. Tatsuya's question was about which level the prediction Kazama had just relayed had come from.

"Ah, this is General Saeki's analysis."

Kazama's answer was not what Tatsuya had expected. Apparently, this analysis was internal to the 101st and wasn't public. This made him adjust his own estimation of the likelihood of imminent military conflict much higher.

The conclusion came from a distinguished veteran officer, without being filtered to avoid upsetting some politician. It was, in a word, *raw* analysis, devoid of the usual bias that came from worrying about political ramifications or public opinion. Tatsuya didn't hope the prediction was true, of course, but he wasn't the sort of person who could embrace baseless optimism.

"While the Ten Master Clans are an organization dedicated to protecting the rights of magicians, they won't shirk their duty to national defense. On that count, the Yotsuba family interests and the military's are aligned."

"Given that I won't involve you in anything unrelated to national defense, I don't expect you'll be put under any undue obligations. I look forward to another productive year with you, Tatsuya." Echoing his earlier sentiment, Kazama brought their conversation to an end.

Once his meeting with Kazama was over, Tatsuya had planned to pay his respects to Sanada, Yanagi, and Yamanaka. However,

Yamanaka wasn't on base, and Sanada and Yanagi were apparently indisposed. As Tatsuya hesitated over whether to find somewhere to wait for a while or return home, Fujibayashi invited him to the officers' café.

It was 10:50 AM—a bit early for lunch but the perfect time for a coffee break. Being so soon after New Year's, the brigade hadn't continued its training in earnest, so the café was quite lively.

Holiday notwithstanding, the brigade was on duty, so every officer was in uniform. Fujibayashi, too, wore her rear echelon female officer's uniform. Tatsuya's three-piece suit stood out in marked contrast. If he'd put on the trench coat he carried in one hand, he might have felt less awkward, but at the moment, he felt strangely conspicuous.

Fujibayashi regarded his self-consciousness with amusement in her eyes. "So even you get bashful sometimes, eh, Tatsuya?"

Tatsuya didn't bother with any bluster, but he did return Fujibayashi's gaze somewhat sullenly. "I prefer not to stick out."

She nearly laughed out loud at the retort. "Ah, so this is a real disaster for you, isn't it?"

"What else could I do? I could hardly refuse."

Fujibayashi peered at him like she was trying to read his mind. "Does that go for your engagement, too?"

"Naturally."

"You're unhappy?"

"Like I said, I didn't have much of a choice in the matter. Just because I'm ordered to marry someone I've thought of as a sister my whole life doesn't mean my feelings can instantly change. I understand the need for Miyuki to be engaged, so I didn't refuse, but…"

This was a front. Tatsuya had accepted the role not because it was necessary but because he couldn't bear to push Miyuki away.

That was something anyone who knew the two well enough could have guessed, so it wasn't hard for Fujibayashi to see the truth, but she didn't say anything to tease him. "'The need to be engaged,' huh?"

Tatsuya looked at Fujibayashi curiously but didn't put his question into words. Given her age, he could easily imagine how much her relatives were probably pressuring her to get married.

But Fujibayashi plunged right into the topic Tatsuya was trying to delicately avoid. "It's gotten really obnoxious lately. 'Just get married already!' I mean, I know I'm not getting any younger, but c'mon…"

Given the modern tendency for magicians to marry young, it wasn't hard to guess that Fujibayashi's family was embarrassed that she wasn't there yet—which was all the more reason for Tatsuya to say nothing.

Knowing the reason why she hadn't married, Tatsuya couldn't let himself say anything thoughtless.

But today, Fujibayashi was determined to step on every land mine Tatsuya was trying to avoid. "I'm well aware, you know? I know I need to sort out my feelings. I can't just stay hung up on him forever—he wouldn't want that for me, either."

Fujibayashi's talk was starting to draw curious looks from other officers in the café, which made Tatsuya even more uncomfortable.

In 2092, Fujibayashi had lost the man she was about to marry in the battle of Okinawa. The engagement had been arranged by their parents, but nevertheless she had been unable to get over the loss.

He had only just received his commission as an officer. Okinawa had been his first assignment, and it was where he was killed in action. His death had been what made Fujibayashi abandon her burgeoning career as a researcher to walk the path of a uniformed officer. She didn't seem to resent the military for his death—perhaps she had decided at some point that she would perform his duty in his stead.

Tatsuya wasn't entirely sure, and she had never elaborated. What he did know was that Fujibayashi hadn't moved on from her fiancé, and her environment wasn't making that any easier.

When Fujibayashi finally noticed Tatsuya's discomfiture, she hastily apologized. "Oh! God, I'm sorry… You don't need to hear me complaining like this, Tatsuya."

"Not at all. I'm sure your family is merely worried about you," was all he could manage as a reply.

Just as Yakumo had said, rumors about Tatsuya and Miyuki spread like wildfire throughout the magician community.

"Shizuku, wait, is that true?!"

"…It has to be," said Shizuku reluctantly, looking away from her friend Honoka, who stood up out of her chair across the table from her.

"Miyuki's gonna be the next head of the Yotsuba family?!"

"Mm-hmm."

Honoka shakily slumped back down to her seat. On the table between the two of them were two cups of black tea and a wide variety of colorful, bite-size cookies and sweets.

It was Sunday, January 6. Shizuku and Honoka were enjoying tea in the dining room of the Kitayama home—although the mood was not exactly pleasant.

Since Honoka had gone to the trouble of coming over to socialize (although it had been Shizuku who'd invited her), Shizuku didn't relish having this conversation with her, but she thought it was preferable to seeing Honoka suddenly find out the next time she saw Tatsuya and Miyuki.

Just as Shizuku had predicted, the news came as a major shock to Honoka, whose gaze wandered about as she sat at the table.

But surprisingly, Honoka didn't remain dazed for long. "Miyuki is…huh…" she murmured, seemingly accepting reality and fixing her eyes firmly on Shizuku. "Okay, that was a surprise, but I can kinda see it. And with their talent and ability, it makes sense that they're both in the Ten Master Clans and Yotsubas to boot."

Honoka gave off a lonely vibe but laughed it off with an expression that made it seem like a weight had been lifted.

"So who did you hear that from? Your aunt? Your uncle?"

"Apparently, the Yotsuba family sent notice to all the Numbered families through the Magic Association. My mom found out through an old contact she has."

"I see. Maybe if my dad was home, he would've told me."

Honoka's father worked as the subordinate of a certain prominent member of a Numbered family. This news hadn't been designated secret, so there was a good chance that it was a source of gossip at his workplace.

For the first time, Shizuku was glad that Honoka's father was away. He didn't know about his daughter's crush. It seemed all too possible that he could've idly mentioned Tatsuya and Miyuki's engagement, catching Honoka by surprise and leaving her with no one around to support her.

Not that this situation was an easy one for Shizuku to manage. She knew she wasn't good at consoling people, which made it hard for her to figure out what to say in the first place.

"Honoka."

"Hmm?"

But…I've got to tell her.

Honoka might well cry. No—she was definitely going to cry. And when she did, Shizuku felt a profound conviction that she was the only one Honoka could really cry in front of.

If Shizuku had felt any other way, she would've done anything to escape this conversation.

"The truth is, that's not all my mom heard."

"There's more? What?"

Shizuku took a breath and said it all at once. "She heard that Miyuki and Tatsuya aren't siblings but cousins. Apparently, not even Miyuki and Tatsuya themselves knew that. So—Tatsuya was chosen as Miyuki's fiancé."

"No…" Honoka's face froze, but she soon smiled. "Oh, come on, Shizuku. Lay off the bad jokes. April Fools' isn't for another three months."

Honoka waited for Shizuku to laugh with her or at least make a sheepish expression and say something like, "You got me."

But Shizuku merely looked back at Honoka glumly.

"C'mon, Shizuku, you can stop kidding around now." Though she was still smiling, there was fear in Honoka's eyes as she pushed Shizuku to reveal the trick.

But Shizuku's voice remained serious. "Honoka…"

"…It's…true?" Honoka asked, trembling.

"…Yeah," Shizuku confirmed hoarsely.

Honoka shot to her feet and tried to run from the dining room, but Shizuku quickly caught up to her. "Honoka!"

"Let me go!" Honoka twisted her body. She didn't know who was holding onto her—nor did she know where she wanted to go or what she would do when she got there. Compelled by survival instinct to flee from the source of her fear, she blindly focused all her strength in her effort to shake free from Shizuku.

"Aaah!"

A cry. The sound of a body hitting the table. The sound of the table's legs creaking. The sound of a chair flipping over. The sound of scattering silverware and breaking dishes.

"…Nnngh."

Finally, a moan of pain brought Honoka to her senses. She hastily looked back to see Shizuku lying beside an overturned chair. Just past her on the floor was a mess of broken cups and saucers.

"Shizuku?! I-I'm sorry! Are you okay?!" Forgetting all about her crying—although now she was near tears for a different reason—Honoka hurried to Shizuku's side.

"I'm fine," said Shizuku, taking Honoka's offered hand but standing up mostly on her own. "Just a little banged up. I'm not seriously hurt." Her statement was meant both for Honoka and for the several maids who'd come rushing in at the sound of the commotion.

As though to reassure them, Shizuku showed no evidence of pain in her expression. She merely looked down at the sleeve of the dress she wore and faintly furrowed her brow. A significant splatter of milk tea was now soaking into the sleeve of her dress.

"Seems I did get a bit on me. I'll go change in my room."

"Ah, miss, let me help you—," offered one of the maids, but Shizuku cut her off flatly.

"No need. Please clean this up instead."

The maids of the house were well aware that the young lady of the house preferred to do her own dressing and bathing, so they did not attempt to offer any more help and quickly set about following Shizuku's orders. "Yes, miss."

"Honoka, you can come with me."

"O-okay," said Honoka, meekly accepting Shizuku's words without any further thought. The shock of having thrown her—a bit of an overstatement, but still—into the table and onto the floor seemed to have overwritten the bewildering news she'd heard immediately prior.

By the time they arrived at Shizuku's room, Honoka had calmed down considerably. Once they were alone, the first thing Honoka did was apologize.

"Shizuku, I, uh…I'm really sorry. I shouldn't have lost control like that…"

"Don't worry about it. It's not like I was injured badly, and I don't think it's even going to bruise."

As she spoke, Shizuku had already shed her dress and was dropping her slip to the floor. As she bent over, Honoka could see the left hip, shoulder, and elbow that Shizuku had banged in her fall. Shizuku's pale skin was faintly reddened, but it did indeed seem unlikely to bruise.

"You can just sit wherever, Honoka," said Shizuku as she put on a flowing maxi dress.

Honoka looked around the room, then plopped herself down on the edge of Shizuku's large bed.

"There we go," said Shizuku upon finishing her changing. She sat down next to Honoka.

Even sitting, she was taller than Honoka, so she naturally ended up looking down at her as the two regarded each other.

"Honoka, are you okay?"

The words triggered a renewed swell of grief. Tears welled up in Honoka's eyes, and Shizuku wrapped her arms around the girl's shoulders.

"Is it really true that Tatsuya and Miyuki are cousins?"

"Yes."

"And that they're engaged?" Honoka wailed through her tears.

Shizuku squeezed Honoka tightly in reply.

"It's...it's not *fair*..." As though a dam inside her had broken, Honoka began to sob in earnest. "Tatsuya...said she was his sister... Miyuki...she said we were friends, too..."

Shizuku wordlessly drew her knees up and held Honoka's head to her chest. As Honoka's crying died down—she hadn't stopped so much as exhausted herself—Shizuku brought her lips close to her friend's ear.

"Honoka, you have three choices."

Honoka's body stirred with something besides a sob. Once Shizuku was certain her friend was hearing her, she continued.

"First, you can give up on Tatsuya. That's probably the least painful path."

Honoka gave no reaction, instead waiting for the other suggestions.

"Second, you can stay the course and pursue Tatsuya. I think Tatsuya really did believe Miyuki was his sister. The fact that they're not came as a huge shock to both of them, I'm sure."

"...You think so?" murmured Honoka tearfully.

"I do," replied Shizuku, carefully avoiding phrases like *probably* or *I think so*. "Miyuki has loved Tatsuya as a man for a long time, but Tatsuya has only ever thought of her as his sister. The fact that they're to be married must be awkward for him."

"But they're engaged now..."

"Only because they couldn't refuse. This wasn't a decision they made on their own, so your chances aren't zero."

Rather than saying Honoka had a chance, Shizuku very specifically said that her chances weren't zero. Even in her current condition, Honoka understood what that meant. "…And my third choice?"

Shizuku took a breath, then after a brief hesitation, blurted out, "…Your third choice is to become Tatsuya's mistress."

"His mistress?!" At the unexpected word, Honoka raised her tear-streaked face to look at Shizuku.

"Not immediately, of course. Miyuki won't become the head of the Yotsuba clan right away, either, and I imagine their marriage is a ways off as well. Your becoming his mistress would be after Tatsuya married Miyuki."

"But a *mistress*…"

"Could you not stand to know you were sharing him?"

"That's not—! …But maybe it would be better than not having him at all…" Honoka buried her red face in Shizuku's chest again.

"Tatsuya has an extremely special type of magic. I'm sure the Yotsuba family wants him to pass on those genes to many children." Shizuku wrapped her arms around Honoka and held her close. "The first choice will be the least painful for you. The second, if it doesn't work out, still means you wouldn't be hurt past that. But the third option, even if it goes well, could mean lifelong wounds that never heal. Not just for you but for Miyuki as well."

"…"

"I think you should take the first path, Honoka. But it's your choice to make."

Shizuku knew it was a cruel thing to ask of Honoka. But if she left Honoka alone, she was terrified that her friend would sink deeper and deeper into her desolation and never rise out of it.

And if that happened, Shizuku was even more terrified that eventually Honoka would start to long for death.

Shizuku said nothing more, waiting for Honoka's reply.

"…I can't give up," finally came the answer. "I just can't. Not yet. But I can't stand the thought of not being the one he loves the most, either. If I have to hurt Miyuki, I'm ready for that, but I could never go on hurting her again and again."

The words pained Shizuku to hear—but she was also somehow relieved. "So—"

"I choose the second path. Until there's no chance at all, I'll keep pursuing him. …Although probably not right away."

Shizuku furrowed her brow at the muttered end of Honoka's declaration, not certain what to make of it.

"…I think I'm going to need a little break."

"A break from love?"

"A break from being *in* love."

Her face still pressed against Shizuku's chest, Honoka chuckled.

Shizuku pulled away from Honoka and composed herself there on the bed, laughing shyly.

[2]

On January 8, the first day of the new semester, Tatsuya, Miyuki, and Minami arrived at the school half an hour earlier than usual.

This wasn't because of an opening ceremony or anything of the sort. And although the three were all members of the student council, it wasn't as though they needed to arrive early in order to perform some special function at the beginning of the term.

No, the reason they arrived early was due to a request from the school. The previous day, Tatsuya and Miyuki had each received a message requesting that they appear at the principal's office before school started.

The e-mail had arrived just after noon. At the time, Miyuki had been at home, while Tatsuya was working at FLT. As a result, they hadn't been able to discuss the summons until after dinner, whereupon they quickly arrived at a conclusion: It had to be about the Yotsuba announcement.

It would be an opportunity for them to explain themselves, along with some scolding for providing false information to the school and a remonstration that despite being engaged, they were still expected to maintain appropriate conduct—that sort of thing.

Their prediction was not incorrect.

In front of Tatsuya and Miyuki sat the vice principal, Yaosaka, and past him on the other side of a large, heavy desk was the principal, Azuma Momoyama. Minami, meanwhile, was in her own classroom, as the e-mail had only been addressed to Tatsuya and Miyuki.

"Now then, you're saying that you never deliberately provided false information?"

"That is correct. It was what was recorded in the family registry, so I believed it myself."

Momoyama's face darkened into a slight frown, although it was unclear whether that was out of irritation at Tatsuya's decision to speak in a rigid tone like he was delivering a military report or at his total lack of fear or nervousness.

Sensitive to the principal's displeasure, Yaosaka nervously contributed to the questioning. "So you're saying the family register itself was falsified? If it's determined that your guardian willfully provided falsified application documents, your school records could be expunged."

"I believe you have already received a letter from my father detailing his explanation and apology."

"We have received that, yes. But are we really to believe this went unnoticed for seventeen years?"

"My father has no interest in me. Upon reflection, that may be because I was never his biological son."

Yaosaka's expression didn't shift, not even at Tatsuya's blunt statement. Such situations were not uncommon—whether in the past or present—which made Tatsuya's story that much more believable.

"Principal, sir, I don't believe there's anything irregular in Mr. Shiba's explanation here," the vice principal went on.

Momoyama did not immediately reply.

"The public data, beginning with the family register, has already been corrected. Considering the family's special circumstances, I don't think there's any need for punishment. What do you think, sir?"

"I understand the situation," Principal Momoyama declared with a grave nod. "And indeed, you two are not responsible. No place of education should ever punish the innocent. However, do not forget that this was a serious error that could have resulted in the expunging of your entire school records. I will need to have a serious talk with your guardians about this."

"Understood." Tatsuya and Miyuki both executed neat bows.

"Now, as far as you two being engaged goes, I expect you to continue to uphold the morals of this school. Given your circumstances, I won't oppose your cohabitation."

The siblings bowed again to Momoyama.

Yaosaka added a final remonstration: "It was previously permitted because you were siblings, and the only reason that isn't changing now is because you are engaged. See that you don't forget that."

"Yes, sir."

With that, their interrogation in the principal's office was concluded.

The lecture ended earlier than they'd expected—but Tatsuya arrived at Class 2-E's classroom a bit later than usual, which was probably why Erika had taken up a post in a window of the classroom that faced the hallway. "Hey, there he is!" she cried.

Hearing that Tatsuya hadn't arrived yet, Leo had returned briefly to his own Class 2-F classroom, but as Tatsuya passed by, he stuck his head into the hall and called out to him. "Hey, Tatsuya. Been a while."

Tatsuya paused. "Hey, Erika, Leo. It sure has." He put Erika's name first, since he had the vague feeling that if he didn't, she'd pout.

"When did you get back to Tokyo?" she asked, which was when Tatsuya remembered that he'd promised to get in touch with her once he'd wrapped up other business.

"The fourth. Sorry I didn't check in."

Tatsuya didn't forget things. More accurately, he simply failed to think of them in the first place. In this particular case, he hadn't had a spare moment to remember his promise.

"Nah, it's fine. I bet you were pretty busy, right?"

"You know he was—and it's only going to get worse. No need to bother with us until things calm down a bit."

Leo's words took Tatsuya by surprise. It wouldn't have been surprising for Erika to know the contents of the letter the Yotsuba family had sent to the Magic Association—the Chibas were one of the many Numbered families to whom the Yotsubas had directed the announcement.

But Leo was unconnected to the Japanese magic world. He'd inherited his magic ability from his grandfather, a refugee from Germany. He had no blood relation to any Japanese magicians, so he shouldn't have had any line on information from the Magic Association of Japan nor connections that would pass its rumors on to him.

Had the news traveled so far already? Tatsuya would soon have his answer.

The moment he entered the classroom, the gazes of all his classmates focused on him, then quickly dispersed.

Tatsuya had a good guess what everybody was thinking, but he decided he might as well at least *pretend* things were normal. He took his seat next to Mizuki and greeted her. "Good morning."

"Ah, er, um, good morning..." As he expected, she immediately looked away after replying. Her reaction told him everything he needed to know.

Tatsuya turned away and raised the terminal built into his desk.

Both Erika, with her elbow still propped in the window frame, and Leo, leaning against the glass in the hallway, watched their friend with interest.

Tatsuya glanced in their direction with an expression on his face that said *don't worry about it*.

Mikihiko didn't appear in Class E's classroom that morning.

◇ ◇ ◇

By the end of morning classes, Tatsuya's classmates were still walking on eggshells.

Tatsuya had never been one for idle conversation, but this was the first time no one had said anything to him all morning. He was competent in a variety of subjects, so having a classmate ask him for help with one problem or another was a daily occurrence.

What bothered Tatsuya was that everyone's glances carried no malice or hostility. If they'd been obviously ostracizing him, then he simply would have banished any consideration of their existence from his mind.

Tatsuya was not a misanthrope, but at the same time, he didn't particularly care about people—himself included.

The truth was that the only person he needed was Miyuki. He wasn't very concerned about what became of everyone else. A pleasant life was simply easier to achieve with the help of others, and that was all. That being the case, in the absence of malice directed at him, Tatsuya preferred to maintain good relationships with the people around him.

But given the current circumstances, he determined that there was no rational action he could take.

"Mizuki, I'm going to the student council room. If anybody asks, tell them that's where I am, would you?"

"Er, okay!" Mizuki said, startled at the sound of his voice. Scaring her would just have to be the price he paid to make it clear he wasn't storming out of the classroom.

He'd told the truth when he said he was going to the student council room. But when he got there, he didn't even make it through the door before pulling a U-turn.

Honoka and Shizuku were inside.

The door wasn't open, and he wasn't using Elemental Sight, but he could still tell when someone was on the other side of a single door. If they'd been like Tatsuya and deliberately minimized their presence—something that had become largely unconscious to him—maybe he wouldn't have noticed, but as it was, regular students didn't bother to hide. These two girls were no exception.

Honoka was on the student council, so it was not at all strange for her to be present. Shizuku was often in the room as well. But for both of them to be there on this particular day was unexpected.

Also unexpected was the fact that Miyuki *wasn't* there.

So Tatsuya instantly turned on his heel and left.

Honoka and Shizuku were in the student council room to escape the curious gazes they were receiving in the dining hall. It was well-known around the school that they were both close to Miyuki, and more than a few of the junior girls knew all about Honoka's crush on Tatsuya.

Miyuki had avoided the dining hall for the same reason—all the more so as she was the subject of the swirling rumors. As the student council president, she often ate in the student council room, and Tatsuya had assumed she would do so that day. He'd imagined that if anything, Honoka and Shizuku would want to avoid being in a room with Miyuki, but it was Miyuki who'd gone elsewhere apparently.

Especially given the dire pronouncements drilled into them by the principal and vice principal, Tatsuya had planned on avoiding eating lunch with his sister for the time being. That necessity had also occurred to Miyuki, since when he suggested it to her after they'd left the principal's office, she'd agreed, albeit with a displeased expression.

Thus, they hadn't arranged any particular rendezvous spot. But upon turning his attention inward for a moment, he soon realized exactly where she had to be. It wouldn't have been hard to guess where she'd gone off to, either, but Tatsuya merely discerned her location, then headed in that direction.

He opened the door to the roof, and there was Miyuki.

There wasn't any snow falling today, but the temperature was still barely above freezing. No other student would contemplate hanging out on the roof in such frigid weather. It was the perfect place to be alone.

"Ah, Tatsuya. I've been waiting."

Well, not just alone—together, alone. Which had been what Miyuki wanted all along.

"If you'd contacted me, I would've come straight here, you know," he offered.

She smiled softly. "I had no doubt whatsoever that you would know where to find me."

The warmth of that smile suffused Tatsuya's body. It wasn't his imagination, either; it was Miyuki's magic.

"You haven't had lunch yet, have you? Come sit." Miyuki gestured to her side. She was sitting on a bench that had room for three. He had planned on sitting next to her anyway, so he accepted her suggestion without hesitation.

Miyuki took two boxes—a larger and a smaller—out of the thermal pack that rested on her lap. The smaller she kept, and the larger she gave to Tatsuya. They were, of course, bento boxes.

"You made us lunch?"

"Yes, I did it while you were at your morning training. I figured we would need our own food today."

Now that he thought about it, Minami had been carrying a rather large bag when the three of them had walked to school.

"Huh. Thanks, Miyuki."

It occurred to Tatsuya that since she hadn't told him about her lunch plans ahead of time, her effort could easily have gone to waste. But then he realized why she hadn't—Miyuki had prepared the lunches because she'd anticipated that they wouldn't want to eat in either the cafeteria or the student council room. And she hadn't said anything about it because she hadn't wanted to create a self-fulfilling prophecy. Tatsuya was sure of it.

"No need to thank me. But look—we can have lunch together after all."

Tatsuya smiled uneasily at Miyuki's barb. "If you'd told me you'd made lunch for us, I wouldn't have suggested eating separately."

"Hmm, I wonder." Miyuki's reply sounded dissatisfied, but she was obviously in good spirits. Regardless of the circumstances, she was clearly happy that they could eat together.

But Tatsuya could tell that to some extent, she was putting on a brave face.

"Yes, it is. Anyway, can I eat now?"

"Yes, by all means."

Having received permission, Tatsuya took the lid off the bento box.

Miyuki smiled impishly and thrust her own chopsticks into Tatsuya's open box. "In fact, there should be no problem with my feeding you, should there?"

Carefully balancing the bento box in her own lap so that it didn't fall, Miyuki turned to face Tatsuya, bringing a piece of one of the fried side dishes in the lunch near his mouth.

"Don't mind if I do," he replied calmly, carefully taking the bite so that his lips didn't touch Miyuki's chopsticks.

Miyuki's face reddened as she watched him. She hastily recomposed herself, opening her own bento box, which gave her an excuse to look away from him.

She'd been hoisted by her own petard.

"You always make really good lunches, Miyuki," Tatsuya said, glancing aside at her to make certain she'd heard. He decided keep his teasing to a minimum, although the line *Aren't you going to feed me any more?* very nearly made it out. "It's nice to be able to be alone with you, but being out under the winter sky like this just feels so chilly. If we can find an empty classroom somewhere, we should use it starting tomorrow."

"Are you sure we should…be alone together again tomorrow?"

"I think that'd be best for a little while. Not when we have student council duties, of course."

This of course flew directly in the face of what he'd said in the morning, but Miyuki didn't argue. "I'll try and find a room today, then," she said resolutely, clenching her fist in determination.

"I'll do the same, so don't push yourself too hard," Tatsuya offered with a smile, trying to calm his suddenly fiery sister.

"So how was Class A?" Tatsuya broached the subject after they'd finished eating and replaced the lids on their bentos.

"It was rather awkward, which I suppose was unavoidable. Everyone was keeping their distance and watching me, and if I tried to talk to anyone, they were really vague and roundabout."

"Yeah, nobody initiated a conversation with me, either."

"Also, Honoka and Shizuku didn't say hello to me."

Hearing this, Tatsuya frowned. "...Were they angry?"

"Well, when I talked to them, they at least answered me, but... yes, I suppose they're avoiding me, at the very least," Miyuki muttered, downcast.

"Well, if they're not giving us the silent treatment, then it's probably okay, right? I think they'll understand that we didn't have any choice in the matter."

"...I hope you're right." Miyuki smiled uncertainly.

"Try to assume it is. Even if it isn't, there's no point in worrying about it." Tatsuya put his hand to Miyuki's cheek.

Miyuki laid her hand upon Tatsuya's and closed her eyes. "I'll try."

"Time might settle all this. It's too early to start being pessimistic."

"You're right...but that goes for you, too, Tatsuya," Miyuki said, peering at him mischievously. "Knowing you, I bet you're thinking of just leaving your friends alone until time settles *your* problems, too, right? Well, I happen to think that sometimes it's good to take the initiative."

Tatsuya chuckled, chagrined, conceding the point. "You got me there."

Upon returning home from school, Tatsuya called the Yotsuba head's direct line.

Until last New Year's Eve, Tatsuya hadn't been allowed to call Maya's direct line, but now she was—publicly, anyway—his mother. No one could object to him calling her.

Next to Tatsuya was a meek-looking Miyuki. Normally around this time, she would be busy preparing dinner, but she understood that there were other things that took priority. She'd left the evening's dinner preparation to Minami.

"*Sorry to keep you waiting. This is perfect timing for you to call, Tatsuya,*" Maya said.

It was actually the second time he'd tried to call. On the first, Hayama had appeared on the visiphone's screen. He'd instructed Tatsuya to call back in twenty minutes, which he had done. "Were you busy?" he asked.

"*Let's talk about why you're calling, first,*" Maya said. Tatsuya was very interested in what *business* Maya might have with him and Miyuki, but he obediently followed the woman's lead.

"This morning, Miyuki and I were called to the principal's office," Tatsuya began and then related the rest of what had happened during the meeting.

"*So Mr. Momoyama gave you a stern talking-to, eh...?*" murmured Maya, an amused lilt in her voice. It sounded like she had some sort of personal acquaintance with him. "*Well, anyway, thank you for the report. You and Miyuki don't need to do anything for now.*"

"Understood." Tatsuya and Miyuki bowed to the visiphone's camera.

"*And now I have something to report to you,*" began Maya as the two raised their heads.

Tatsuya listened attentively, realizing that this wasn't going to be about a new mission or duty for him.

"We've received a formal notice of protest filed by the Ichijou family via the Magic Association."

"Why would the Ichijou family protest?" Miyuki asked. Her facial expression was composed, but both Tatsuya and Maya could tell that beneath it was fierce indignation.

"It gives me no pleasure to explain," Maya began, unruffled to be the bearer of bad news. Not only was she not sparing Miyuki's feelings, she seemed almost amused at the girl's defiance. *"The Ichijou are protesting on the grounds that you are too closely related to marry. They insist that the genes of those with magical talent are valuable national assets and that we cannot risk harming the next generation by passing down any genetic abnormalities."*

"That's—!" Miyuki raised her voice, but Tatsuya interrupted her.

"I'm sure that wasn't all there was to it. Avoiding genetic disorders isn't a concern limited to magicians. That's why there are laws about that sort of thing."

"That wasn't the only reason, but it was certainly the most prominent one."

"And by the same token, not even the Ten Master Clans have the right to protest a lawful engagement. No doubt the Ichijou family had something else they also wanted to say, correct?"

Maya nodded with a satisfied smile. *"Got it in one. As clever as always, Tatsuya."*

For Tatsuya's part, he took no particular pleasure in the praise. "So what did they have to say?"

"Well, actually…they proposed an engagement between their oldest son and Miyuki."

"Refuse them!" Miyuki immediately cried out.

"Miyuki—," Tatsuya began to rebuke, but Maya cut him off.

"It's fine, Tatsuya," she said gently. *"Miyuki's anger is understandable. I also think it's untoward for them to respond to the announcement of your engagement with a proposal of their own."*

"So you'll tell them we refuse…?" asked Miyuki hopefully.

But Maya's reply was not so clearly affirmative: *"Not right away, Miyuki. I'm not going to tell them anything immediately."*

"Won't that weaken our position?" asked Tatsuya.

Maya nodded understandingly. *"I don't intend to delay forever. But you two don't need to worry about this."*

"You're telling us not to do anything rash."

"Right you are. You two just keep getting along *with each other the way you always have."*

"Aunt Maya…" murmured Miyuki, looking askance, embarrassed by what Maya's emphasis of the words *getting along* meant.

"Understood," Tatsuya said without batting an eye, giving the camera a polite bow.

There was no real change in the way Miyuki and Tatsuya's classmates treated them on the second day of the new semester. Their fellow students kept their distance and watched them with undisguised curiosity. Still, it wasn't the kind of problem that was going to improve in just a single day—although one day was more than enough time for it to get worse.

Miyuki had always been something of a campus icon. Her beauty and skill alone were enough to make her rather difficult to approach. Her recently revealed lineage only added to that. It was no surprise that even older students acted diffident around her.

On the other hand, there was Tatsuya, toward whom more than a few students harbored a secret fear.

Fear. Anxiety. Terror. The apprehension, the trepidation, the dread one felt toward an unnaturally powerful warrior.

With Tatsuya's direct connection to *the* Yotsuba clan now public, that feeling only grew. People were terrified to approach him, but their fear made it impossible for them to ignore him, too. This manifested in generally distant and standoffish treatment.

But the interest the young high school students held for them wasn't just for those reasons. The scandals of the rich and famous have always been a subject of intense public interest. It would have been impossible to stop the prurient interest aroused by the story of these too-close siblings who were revealed to be cousins now engaged and cohabitating.

It was morning, before class started. Minami had just arrived in the Class 1-C classroom when she was immediately surrounded by a mass of students, most of whom were girls.

"I told you, nothing's different with them."

Minami had repeated this answer many times since the semester had started. Other variations of the answer included *Nothing like that is happening*, *I'm not at liberty to say*, and *I'm sorry, but I can't answer that*.

"What? But they're together *all day!*"

"Right, so when they have a day off…like, you know…"

A gleeful squeal arose from the crowd. By contrast, Minami sighed lightly. "As I said, Tatsuya and Miyuki are doing nothing of the sort." She was perfectly aware that her honest answer was falling on deaf ears, but she didn't want to risk a silence that would be interpreted as agreement.

Then, as though rewarding her patience, the next question was a change of subject:

"That reminds me, Sakurai, up through December you were calling Tatsuya and Miyuki 'brother' and 'sister,' weren't you? Does that mean you're part of the Yotsuba clan, too?"

The chatter from the classmates surrounding Minami came to an abrupt stop. They all seemed to hold their breath, watching Minami intently to see how she would answer.

"I formerly referred to Tatsuya and Miyuki that way at Tatsuya's request. And the Yotsuba clan is, er, providing me support…"

Minami very nearly said the true answer, *I serve the Yotsuba clan*, but managed to change her wording at the last second. But her hesitation made it sound very much like she was hiding something.

"Really? Is that true?"

"Yes, really."

Since the fact was that she was lying, her attempt to refute their skepticism was feeble. Of course, if she'd protested more vociferously, that also would've been taken as evidence that she was being deceptive.

"Huh, so the Yotsuba family does stuff like that, too."

The work of a magician was dangerous. It wasn't uncommon for the daughter of a magician who'd died in the line of duty to be taken in as a ward or assistant by another family. There were such students at First High—and even here in Class C, which explained why no one found Minami's explanation of support questionable or suspicious.

"But the Yotsuba family supporting you doesn't mean that you have no connection to them at all, does it?"

But that didn't mean it was normal to ask someone in Minami's position about every single little detail of her life. "Um, well…"

It was the arrival of the class leader who rescued the tongue-tied Minami from her classmates' insensitive questions. "Okay, everybody, class is starting soon! We'll get demerits if we're not all in our seats!"

In response to Kasumi's loud interruption, one of the girls checked the time on her terminal. "Saegusa, it's not—"

Kasumi cut her off with a smile, repeating herself. "I said *soon*, didn't I?"

"O-okay."

Not so much convinced by Kasumi's logic as overwhelmed by her smile, the girls surrounding Minami peeled off in twos and threes as they returned to their seats. Kasumi watched them go, her arms folded, then sniffed and headed for her own seat.

"Um—thank you, Saegusa," said Minami from behind her.

Kasumi looked over her shoulder. "No problem. I hate that kind of thing," she said with a quick wink.

The next break between classes passed without another human wall forming around Minami, but this was only because it was a practical skills class, and the need to move to another classroom meant there was no time for interrogation. She would not be so lucky during lunch. More than one or two of her classmates was planning on following her to the dining hall and questioning her very thoroughly.

At the bell signaling the end of morning classes, more than half the population of Class 1-C stood up.

But Kasumi was one step ahead of them. "Sakurai, you're going to the student council room, right? Let's go together."

In a sense, it was natural. The seating order of the freshmen was split by gender, then alphabetically. Kasumi's last name was Saegusa, and Minami's was Sakurai, which put Kasumi's seat directly in front of Minami's. It wasn't strange at all that Kasumi would be the first to reach Minami.

Minami's eyes went round in surprise. Her shock was understandable—in the nine months she'd sat behind Kasumi, this was the first time the girl in front of her had ever invited her to do anything.

For her part, Kasumi had never had anything against Minami—she'd just vaguely avoided her since Minami was a relative of Tatsuya's. And then today, this. Minami wasn't the only surprised one.

"C'mon, let's go."

At Kasumi's urging, Minami hastily grabbed the bag containing her bento box and stood.

"Um, Saegusa—" Minami's voice had a questioning tone to it as she matched Kasumi's stride. The two were climbing the stairs that would take them to the student council room.

"What's up?" replied Kasumi, having instantly caught onto Minami's uncertainty.

"I just wanted to thank you again for this morning. But—why did you save me?"

Minami didn't think Kasumi hated her, but neither did she imagine that the girl particularly liked her. And that wasn't just a baseless assumption. It was plain fact that the two girls hadn't shared more than the absolute minimum interaction. Minami herself hadn't taken any initiative to become friendly with Kasumi, either, which was all the more reason she was surprised that Kasumi had come to her rescue today.

"I told you—I hate that kind of thing." The smile Kasumi directed at Minami was a bit awkward. Minami guessed that it was because they weren't at all close or intimate, but the truth was Kasumi was a bit embarrassed about being so frankly told that she'd *saved* someone. "I know how it feels to be in that situation. Even if they're just asking out of honest curiosity, it's really insensitive to the person getting badgered."

"That's true." Minami hadn't been hurt by insensitive questioning so much as she'd been put in the awkward situation of being unable to answer because of her position, but in either case, the problem was the lack of empathy, so her agreement with Kasumi's statement was genuine.

"I mean, I've been through a decent amount of that crap myself." Kasumi suddenly relaxed, letting down her guard in a way she rarely did at school. Perhaps she'd sensed Minami's own empathy.

Kasumi seemed not to have noticed her own ease. Minami's ears pricked up at the sudden shift in her tone, but her well-practiced composure as a servant kept her from reacting in a way Kasumi would have noticed.

Saturday, January 12. The first weekend after the beginning of the new semester.

Saturday classes were limited to mornings, but the dining hall was open for the students participating in extracurricular activities. Erika, Leo, and Mizuki had their clubs, and it was Mikihiko's turn on the discipline committee, so they all met in the dining hall in preparation for the afternoon's activities.

The number of people in their lunch party had dropped by half compared to the previous month. Tatsuya, Miyuki, and Honoka were on the student council, so they just went to the student council room to eat—which was all well and good, but per the intelligence Erika had gotten from Shizuku, Tatsuya and Miyuki had actually been sneaking off to some other undisclosed location to eat since the beginning of the semester.

But it wasn't just the group's dwindling numbers that contributed to the lack of conversation during lunch. A larger factor was Erika—normally quite the conversationalist—who was radiating irritation from every pore on her body.

Mikihiko quickly finished eating and tried to leave, undoubtedly in a hurry to be absolutely anywhere else.

"Now just wait a second, Miki," said Erika, catching him right as he was standing up and preventing his escape.

"What? Why?" he asked, trying to hide his dismay at being thwarted with a prickly tone.

Naturally, Erika would not be cowed by one snappish reply. "Wait until Mizuki finishes eating."

Mikihiko and Erika's exchange was visibly unsettling Mizuki. Eventually, she put her chopsticks down with a full one-third of her plate's contents uneaten.

The four were sitting at a table, with Erika next to Mizuki and directly across from Leo.

Erika looked diagonally across at Mikihiko, then leaned toward him threateningly, her voice raised. "What's your problem, Miki?!"

"What's *my* problem?" Mikihiko shot back, not exactly smoothly.

"Oh, so you're gonna make me say it out loud? Fine, I'll say it!" Erika slammed her palm down onto the table. The sharp, sudden noise drew some attention, but she didn't seem to notice. "I wanna know why you're avoiding Tatsuya!"

There was a moment of silence. Every gaze in the dining hall was on Erika and Mikihiko. Erika continued to ignore the attention, and Mikihiko was too busy fending her off to notice it.

"I'm not…avoiding him."

"Oh, you're gonna deny it now?"

Mikihiko flinched at Erika's accusing look.

"Even this idiot can tell you've been avoiding Tatsuya." Erika's eyes flicked over to Leo.

"Whoa, whoa, why am I the idiot?! But also, Mikihiko—our resident hothead here has a point— Ow!" Leo suddenly yelped. "Geez! What do you have in your shoes?"

Erika had kicked Leo's shin under the table. "They're not steel toed—don't worry."

The acrimonious mood around the table lifted slightly and not just for Mikihiko or Mizuki.

Erika sighed. "Fine. I don't even have the energy for this anymore," she said, taking the opportunity to back off before retreat became impossible. "Whatever. Look, Miki—I don't know why you're avoiding Tatsuya, and I don't particularly care. But just because it turns out he's a Yotsuba doesn't mean you can treat him like this. That's not what friends do."

Erika gave him a pointed look. If she'd just been trying to start a fight, Mikihiko could've kept pushing back. But the seriousness in Erika's gaze made it impossible for him to disguise the guilt he obviously carried over his treatment of Tatsuya.

"…It's not because he's a Yotsuba. Well, I mean, that's only one of the reasons. I'm mad at him for not talking about any of this."

Mikihiko's downcast eyes weren't just angry—there was frustration in them as well.

Erika found herself meeting Leo's eyes.

"C'mon, Mikihiko. That's not exactly fair, is it?" said Leo patiently. "It's not like Tatsuya hid this from us because he wanted to, right? You've got plenty of tradition riding on your shoulders, too, so you should know that as well as anyone."

"Miki," said Erika pointedly, showing no reaction to what Leo had said. "Suppose you'd learned the truth from Tatsuya himself. What would you have done, then?"

Mikihiko was speechless. Or rather, he couldn't find the words to articulate what he wanted to say.

Erika seized the advantage and fired off another shot. "If Tatsuya had told you that he was a direct descendant of the Yotsuba line, would you really have just left it at *Oh, is that so?* Would you have treated him no differently? Seeing the way you're acting now, I find that hard to believe."

Mikihiko had no answer. He couldn't even muster a convenient lie as a deflection.

"The truth is, Miki, you're just terrified of the Yotsuba name."

"...And what about you, Erika?" Mikihiko muttered sullenly, finally summoning some bravado.

But it was a foolish question. No one as open about her own faults as Erika was could be intimidated like that. "Of course I'm terrified of them," she said. "He's one of *the* Yotsubas. If I didn't feel anything, I wouldn't be brave—I'd be a moron. It's not something you can pretend you didn't hear."

"So how can you keep treating him the same way?"

"Because he's my *friend*," Erika snapped, using exactly the same tone with which she'd admitted her own fear. "The Yotsuba clan is scary. It's creepy not knowing what they might pull. But Tatsuya is my friend. Even if I don't trust the Yotsubas, I trust *Tatsuya*. Even if there's a lot he has to hide from us." She pressed forward, looking into

Mikihiko's eyes as she made her point. "And I'll bet there's a dozen or more things you keep secret from us, too."

"That's…"

"Don't deny it. We've been friends for a long time."

"…"

"And I have my own secrets. Lots of them. Things I don't want anyone to know, things I don't ever plan on telling anyone else about."

Mikihiko looked away uneasily. He had an inkling of what Erika didn't want anyone to know about.

"So he didn't confide his secret to you? So what? You're not his wife—of course he didn't."

Mikihiko slumped, dejected. He had no more excuses left. "Why…why is everything so easy for you guys? Erika? Leo? Why is it so straightforward?"

Outside of Mikihiko's view, Erika glanced at Leo.

"Well," Leo said, "for me, it's because I've never had anything to do with the Yotsuba family. I have no idea how scary their magicians are. But I know Tatsuya. I know exactly how scary he is, but I also know that I can totally trust him." He smiled a little sheepishly. "I mean, that's my call. I might be wrong. And if it turns out I am, I can live with that. Tatsuya's my friend. It'd be stupid to change that just because I might've been wrong."

"Leo…you're incredible, you know that?"

Mikihiko wasn't the only one openly staring at Leo. Erika was just as stunned. When she noticed Mikihiko look over to her, she had to hurry to reestablish her composure.

"Is that how it is for you, too, Erika?" asked Mikihiko.

"No, not exactly. It's not like I accepted it right away…but I didn't drag it out over three or four days."

She'd learned of Tatsuya's circumstances the previous February. Perhaps *realized* was a better word, but in any case, the shock was the same. But whatever her differing circumstances, she'd recovered from the psychological shock in under a day.

If she hadn't found the revelation so deeply unsettling, she wouldn't have had so much to say about Mikihiko's attitude. But because she'd overcome it herself, she couldn't stand to watch Mikihiko dithering around and dragging it out.

"…Okay." Mikihiko closed his eyes and was still. It was not the stillness of calm but of intense conflict. "Fine," he said to Erika, opening his eyes. "I think of Tatsuya as a friend, too. So I'll try. Next Monday, I'll treat him like before." There was something almost relieved in his expression.

Erika smiled, satisfied, and looked over to Mizuki next to her. "That goes for you, too, Mizuki."

"Huh?!" Mizuki's reaction came less from the surprise of being suddenly addressed than it did from the shattering of her quiet relief at having been spared the brunt of Erika's frustration.

"I want you to stop keeping Miyuki and Tatsuya at arm's length. Miki said he's going to try, so that means you can do it, too. Right?"

"Okay…"

Erika pushed against Mizuki's noncommittal answer. "You can do it too, *right?*"

"Y-yes. Fine! I'll do it!"

"I'll be giving it a shot, too, Shibata. We're in it together," Mikihiko said encouragingly to Mizuki.

"…Right! We're in it together." Mizuki nodded brightly.

The truth was, Erika's real aim in confronting Mikihiko in front of Mizuki was to get Mizuki heading in the right direction. Erika knew that confronting Mizuki alone about it wouldn't have gone well, but in pushing Mikihiko to promise to repair his friendship with Tatsuya, she had planned to motivate Mizuki to do likewise.

And it had all gone exactly as she'd planned—but she had to look away, unable to stand it as the two (psychologically) clasped their hands together in insufferably mutual encouragement.

◇ ◇ ◇

Thanks to Erika's persuasion (with an assist from Leo), Mikihiko and Mizuki had decided to set aside their bad feelings toward Tatsuya and Miyuki.

However, Honoka's feelings would not be so easily changed.

She had already decided how she would approach Tatsuya henceforth. But her decision had yet to be translated into action, and she hadn't decided how she planned to interact with Miyuki.

Honoka considered Miyuki a friend. And yet, she was also Honoka's greatest rival in love—and she was already two or three steps ahead.

Thanks to Shizuku's counsel, Honoka no longer felt stung by having been misled by Tatsuya and Miyuki. She'd realized that they themselves had been misled, too.

But she still couldn't smile and laugh with them the way she had so naturally before. Honoka's obvious discomfort had prompted Miyuki to be rather awkwardly careful around her, which created a vicious cycle of unease.

Even now, Honoka was heading for the club activities management room in order to escape the student council room. Honoka was the treasurer of the student council. Her job was to take applications for additional funds from each extracurricular club and discuss them with the club management section. There wasn't anything at all odd about her visiting the club activities management room—but even if nobody else found it strange, Honoka herself knew that she was doing it to avoid the awkwardness of being in a room with Miyuki, and this awareness gnawed at her constantly.

The current president of the club management committee was Igarashi, who was also the captain of the boys' section of the same club Honoka was in. Honoka had known him since their first year of high school. He was a boy whose personality was somewhere in the vague space between kind and timid. The phrase *capable of neither harm nor good* applied, though while he occasionally did manage some helpful things, he wasn't the sort of boy who had it in him to cause any trouble.

He wasn't Honoka's type, but his weak personality generally put her at ease. She figured he would be a good person to talk to when she needed a break from feeling so depressed.

Honoka spoke into the intercom next to the door. "This is Mitsui from the student council."

"Come on in," came the answer—not from the intercom speaker but from inside the room as the door opened.

The student who let her in was Takuma Shippou, a freshman in the club management section. Despite being a prominent member of the entering freshman class, Takuma's reputation among his classmates hadn't initially been good, but on a certain day near the end of April, he'd made a dramatic turnaround.

He was no less assertive than before, but his pushiness had vanished. Even as he continued to pursue leadership roles, he kept his self-righteousness well under control and viewed things in a more holistic fashion.

His easily roused emotions were still part of his personality, but when his mistakes were pointed out to him, he quickly acknowledged them and apologized.

Above all, his efforts to actually grow and change were obvious to everybody, and he had earned the trust and sympathy of his classmates.

All of this had led to him being the obvious selection to lead the nine members of the freshman boys' team representing First High in the Nine School Competition.

Thereafter, he continued to extend his influence but without ever growing arrogant. Lately, even junior and senior students were beginning to notice his constant effort.

Honoka herself had once taken a dim view of Takuma after his early aggression toward Tatsuya. But now she didn't have a particularly poor impression of him. She acknowledged him as one of the more capable underclassmen.

"I have an appointment with Igarashi," Honoka said.

"With the president? He just got called away."

Honoka had contacted Igarashi just before she'd left the student council room to tell him she was on her way, but he'd apparently been summoned to deal with some sudden problem. The previous president, Hattori, had instituted a duty rotation system that was supposed to avoid the problems of too much power concentrated at the top, but Igarashi demonstrated the downside of this when someone too easygoing inherited the position.

Honoka muttered to herself that this had better be a coincidence. Despite not being in any state to be worrying about other people, she couldn't help it when her own sensitivity got the better of her like this. In this sense, she was in no position to cast aspersions on Igarashi.

Honoka was about to turn around and leave when a question from Takuma stopped her short. "Was it something urgent?" Takuma asked.

"Yes, but since he's not here, I figured I'd check back later."

Takuma seemed to be on communications duty and was wearing a wireless headset. It was a model that included brain wave–assist functionality.

"Wait just a moment," he said, returning the receiver to his ear and turning to face the terminal built into the tabletop. "This is Shippou at HQ. ...I have Mitsui from the student council here. ...Yes, understood. I'll tell her."

Takuma slipped the headset off his ears again and stood, facing Honoka. "The president says he'll return shortly and asks that you wait."

"Shortly? Like how long?"

"He didn't say specifically, but based on past examples, I would guess around five minutes."

It would take almost five minutes just to go back to the student council room. Honoka didn't want to be there in the first place, so she decided to wait after all.

But as she stood there doing nothing, she couldn't keep her mind from drifting to all the other things she had to do. *Still, the student council room's been pretty empty recently. I bet there's a lot of data processing work piling up...*

It was simply her nature.

It'd go by in a flash if I could just get Tatsuya to help...but I can't ask him with things as awkward as they are now. But Miyuki's supposed to be in charge of task delegation, so she'll probably ask him to do it even if I don't say anything...but won't that make me seem totally unnecessary?! Honoka turned pale at her own wandering thoughts.

"Um, Mitsui...are you feeling all right?" It was the obvious question to ask, given her appearance. Even for the formerly haughty Takuma.

But the un-self-aware Honoka had no idea why she was being asked such a question. "Huh?!" she exclaimed. Upon the interruption of the near-fantastical thoughts her mind had drifted to, she forgot entirely what she'd been thinking about. Her face remained slightly pale but only because it took a few moments to regain its color. "Uh, nothing! It's nothing!"

Any outside observer would have clocked this as a bluff, as did Takuma. He even came to his own conclusion about its cause.

"Um, Mitsui, look..."

"Yes?"

"Well...I'm perfectly aware that this is none of my business, but about Shiba, have you—"

A nervous Honoka tried to cut Takuma off. "Stop right there, Shippou. Just what have you gotten into your head?"

But even if he'd gotten the wrong idea about Honoka feeling unwell, he certainly wasn't mistaken about the reason for her agitation.

Which was why Honoka was so nervous. She didn't want to hear whatever Takuma was about to say.

But then he said it.

"I really think you should give up on Shiba."

"Stop!"

"If you keep this up, you're just going to get hurt!"

Takuma had changed his heart and improved his attitude, but his fundamental ambition was still there. As a magician with high aspirations, his desire to make Honoka an ally—and, if things went well, thereby become part of Shizuku's inner circle—was still very much intact.

But more than that, he was simply attracted to her.

It had happened the day Takuma got into trouble with Kasumi and ended up squaring off against the Saegusa sisters. Honoka had been the only one to show him any kindness, even when he'd been lashing out at anyone and everyone. Although strictly speaking, all she'd done was lean over Takuma after Tomitsuka had knocked him down and ask, "Can you stand?"—but she hadn't lent him her hand to help him to his feet or anything like that.

In his memory, the moment had become more beautiful, although the affection he had for her hadn't gone so far as to become full-blown love. They didn't have many chances to talk, after all.

And then today, by coincidence, Honoka had appeared right in front of him, tormented by her own feelings of unrequited love. It had sent Takuma right off the rails.

"Mitsui, the truth is, I—I—"

Honoka squeezed her eyes shut and clapped her hands over her ears.

Takuma began to reach out toward her hands but got no further.

"Shippou, what are you doing...?" Igarashi's voice stopped Takuma before he spiraled out of control. The president had returned.

Igarashi wasn't alone. Out from behind him stepped Shizuku, who came around to face Honoka, pulling her into a close embrace.

"Shizuku...?"

"That's right," said Shizuku, as though it meant everything was going to be okay now. She stroked Honoka's back over and over. The stiffness began to melt out of Honoka's body.

Still holding her, Shizuku looked back over her shoulder, glaring at Takuma coldly. "What was it you were about to say?" The temperature of her voice matched her eyes.

"I mean…" The phrase Takuma had planned on finishing his sentence with was *I'm worried about you!*

"Taking advantage of somebody in a moment of weakness? You're the worst." Shizuku's accusation wasn't entirely on the mark—but it wasn't totally unjustified, either.

There was nothing Takuma could say in response to that, and he knew it.

"Let's go, Honoka." Shizuku led Honoka out of the club management room.

Takuma didn't say anything to try to stop them.

Igarashi, who'd been ditched right to his face, just stood there, stunned speechless.

That day, Honoka didn't return to her own apartment. She and Shizuku left school separately from Tatsuya and Miyuki as usual, but the moment they arrived at the train station, Shizuku practically ordered Honoka to stay the night at her place.

It wasn't an invitation. This was a mandatory sleepover.

Honoka certainly didn't mind staying over at Shizuku's home. She was perfectly aware of her own tendency to agonize over things endlessly, and she suspected that if she were left alone, she would only sink further into despair, so she was grateful for the offer.

They ate dinner with Shizuku's parents (who returned home atypically early) for the first time in quite a while, then as usual bathed together, where they chattered on about neutral, superficial topics.

However, the room Shizuku took Honoka to after bathing was not the usual one.

Honoka had her own bedroom in the Kitayama home. It was

supposedly a guest room, but for all intents and purposes, it was Honoka's bedroom. It was decorated to her tastes, and the closet was even fully appointed with clothes—including underwear—that fit her.

Yet, Honoka rarely used the room. When she stayed over at the Kitayama home, she normally stayed in Shizuku's room, sleeping with Shizuku in her bed. But today, Shizuku led Honoka to *her* room.

Honoka obediently entered and sat on the bed, and her previously happy face immediately sank into a droop of sadness and pain.

Shizuku sat in front of her, kneeling on a carpet.

Honoka's head was obviously higher, since she was sitting on the bed. Her downcast face met Shizuku's upturned gaze head-on.

"Honoka."

"I know." Honoka averted her eyes by looking even further down. "You probably think I'm pathetic," she said, her voice teetering on the verge of sobs and her lips quivering. "Even though there's nothing to feel sorry for."

"Well, there's that face you're making."

"What…?" Honoka looked up.

Shizuku's gaze continued to fix on Honoka. "You've had that face all week."

"'That face'…?"

"The face of a pitiful girl."

Honoka covered her mouth with her hand, shocked. "No…"

"Shippou was in the right, back there," continued Shizuku with brutal honesty. "Everyone's been watching you from a distance. They see how miserable you've been."

"I never asked for that! I don't want anyone's pity!"

"What you want isn't relevant. People pity others for their own reasons." Shizuku reached up and forced Honoka's wandering eyes to meet her own. "By pitying someone else, they reassure themselves that they're different."

"I'm…I'm not *pitiful*!"

"I know." Shizuku nodded to Honoka's agony, looking steadily into her eyes. "I know that you're not. But not everyone does." Shizuku's gaze didn't waver. "They don't know how determined you are. They don't know how *strong* you are."

Honoka signaled recognition with her eyes.

"And that's because you're not showing them with your actions and attitude."

Shizuku pulled away from Honoka and stood. She towered over her.

"Honoka. On Monday—"

Honoka held her breath nervously.

"—I want you to show me that you're not this pathetic girl."

Without waiting for an answer one way or another, Shizuku left the room.

On Sunday, January 13, Tatsuya went to the FLT research facility where he worked. Despite it not being a workday, there seemed to be just as many people at R & D Section 3, the CAD development center, as usual.

As its name suggested, the facility focused on CAD development, but Tatsuya was not currently being employed in either novel CAD research or CAD-specific software development.

He was working on the design, generation capacity, and model plan for nonmilitary use of the stellar reactor.

The company had no idea Tatsuya was attempting to build such a thing, because Tatsuya had never reported it. This was possible because he wasn't an employee of FLT, but rather a contracted researcher, so he was largely given free rein as long as he kept to his confidentiality agreement.

Because he had his own office in R & D Section 3, if he wanted to work on something in secret, he could easily hide his activities.

Tatsuya hadn't even talked to Ushiyama, his partner in Taurus Silver, about this.

But that didn't mean the section staff's treatment of him had changed.

"Ah, good morning, Prince."

"Prince, good morning."

As he headed for his office, various FLT staffers greeted Tatsuya. They were already fully aware of his connection to the Yotsuba family, because on his first workday of the year, he'd assembled the staff and announced it to them himself.

Nonetheless, the attitude of everyone who called him *Prince* didn't change. R & D Section 3 was a ragtag band of misfits to begin with, and they had little respect for authority, so their reaction to learning he was a magician in the Yotsuba family was mostly *So what?* In any case, Tatsuya was thankful that nobody was being excessively deferential. It let him give his full attention to assembling the planning documents.

The construction planning was for a nonmilitary application of magic—a project called ESCAPES: Extract both useful and harmful Substances from the Coastal Area of the Pacific using Electricity generated by a Stellar reactor. It was meant to be the escape hatch for magicians who'd been originally created as weapons.

It had also originally been meant to be Tatsuya's livelihood after he made his escape from the Yotsuba family. His motivations were slightly different now that he had been acknowledged as a core member of that family, but the importance of the project as a nonmilitary application for magic hadn't changed. The energy from a magically operated nuclear fusion reactor would be a stable source of electricity and fuel and could supply a variety of mineral resources as a by-product, bringing stability to the industrial world. And in doing so, it would guarantee the livelihood of nonmilitary magicians. That was the fundamental thought process behind the project.

With the rise of renewables like solar, wind, and biomass, modern industry had had to adapt to energy availability that varied from year to year based on climate and weather. This was preferable to a society that was dependent on fossil fuels and nuclear fission, of course, both from the perspective of sustainable development and the protection of an environment that made human life possible. However, it was undeniable that energy and fuel availability had become less stable. The national project to develop a system of orbital photovoltaic platforms to supply non-weather-variable energy was another reaction to this reality.

The scheme Tatsuya envisioned had four main parts: First, the stellar reactor would generate electricity and heat. Then, hydrogen gas would be produced via electrolysis. Next, fresh water would be created via reverse osmosis. And finally, both useful and harmful substances would be extracted from the remaining concentrated seawater.

Of course, while Tatsuya had a deep mastery of magic technology, his understanding of industrial engineering remained at the high school level. For technologies outside the stellar furnace itself, he would have to rely on the help of specialists. Nothing in the production of hydrogen, the extraction of fresh water, or the recovery of trace elements from seawater was impossible with magic, but relying on magicians for all that would be too heavy a burden. Treating magicians as mere parts in the machine ran counter to the goal of this project, and it was never Tatsuya's aim to design a production system composed only of magicians.

It ought to be the Magic Association that approaches the nonmagic community about this. The association's name will make it easier to find partners than the Yotsuba name would, and it'll avoid objections from the association itself. The difficulty will be making the specific arrangements, I suppose.

The overall concept was finished. Tatsuya anticipated that the systems surrounding the stellar reactor could be drafted inside three months and specified within six. Beyond that, he recognized he wouldn't be able to proceed alone.

This timeline might be a bit too aggressive, considering that I'm still a high school student...

People might not be willing to work with him because of his youth. At the moment, that was Tatsuya's greatest source of concern.

[3]

It was Monday morning, the beginning of the second week of the new term.

Upon arriving in the Class 2-E classroom, Tatsuya was greeted—as had once been the norm—by Mizuki, who sat next to him.

"Good morning!" she chimed.

"Good morning, Mizuki."

She met Tatsuya's salutation with a smile—albeit a slightly awkward one.

If her smile had been perfectly natural, though, Tatsuya would've found it off-putting. But seeing his classmate forcing herself to be casual, he felt suddenly grateful for his friends.

If he'd been in Mizuki's place, he was sure he'd want to keep his distance from anyone as suspicious as he was. Mizuki wasn't deeply involved with the world of magicians, so it was no surprise that she'd be wary of the dreaded Yotsuba name—especially when it was someone who'd hidden their true identity for close to two years. And yet, here was Mizuki, an ordinary girl, making an effort to reach out to him in friendship. Tatsuya's emotional sensitivity was not so poor that he'd take this for granted.

Just as he took his seat, the hall-facing window immediately to his right rattled open.

"Good morning, Tatsuya!"

Greeting him through the window was Erika. Leo wasn't with her this morning, but Tatsuya avoided pointing that out, remembering how Erika had once angrily rebuked, *Don't pair us up like it's the obvious thing to do!*

And they weren't a couple, after all, so it wasn't particularly odd for them not to be together.

"And morning, Mizuki!" she finished.

"Morning, Erika!"

Mizuki smiled her trademark sunny smile, at which Erika nodded, satisfied. "That's the spirit!"

Noting that Erika's interference had brought about this change in Mizuki's demeanor, Tatsuya ventured to ask, "What's up, Erika? You seem happy."

"Huh? Oh, it's nothing," replied Erika, as Tatsuya had expected.

When morning classes were over, Miyuki stood up and prepared to head to the practicum building to wait for Tatsuya. The practicum building had instruction rooms that were used for group combat training, and it had been their lunchtime spot for the past several days.

It would soon be a week since they'd started secretly having lunch together to avoid prying eyes. Miyuki was happy to get to spend time alone with Tatsuya, but it was a constant, lonely reminder of their inauspicious, uncelebrated relationship.

Just as Miyuki was leaving to meet up with Tatsuya, a voice called out to her from behind.

"Miyuki."

It was Honoka.

"What is it?"

Honoka's face was stiff with nervousness. Although her own expression didn't betray it, Miyuki was nervous, too. It had been about a week since she'd exchanged any words with the girl other than what was needed for official student council business.

In fact, the entirety of Class 2-A was nervous, holding their breath and looking on as Miyuki and Honoka regarded each other.

"It—it's lunchtime, right? Um, want to come to the student council room with me?" Honoka asked.

Miyuki couldn't immediately reply. She herself had wanted to make up, but she'd never imagined that Honoka would take the initiative and approach her first.

Before Miyuki's uncharacteristic silence could be misinterpreted as rejection, Shizuku cut in from the side and, with a few words, came to both Miyuki and Honoka's rescue. "Oh, can I come, too?"

With a bright smile, Miyuki nodded to both of them.

By the time Tatsuya—who'd received a message on his portable terminal—arrived in the student council room, Miyuki, Honoka, and Shizuku were already sitting at a table.

But nobody was holding chopsticks yet. Miyuki's bento box was unopened, and Honoka and Shizuku had nothing in front of them.

"Here he is. Thank you for making it."

"Yes, and come have a seat, Tatsuya."

Miyuki and Honoka both stood and gestured for him to sit. His place was next to Miyuki and directly across from Honoka. Shizuku also stood and went to the room's dining cabinet where her and Honoka's lunch trays had been kept warm.

The four enjoyed a pleasant meal. Honoka and Shizuku provided the table's discussion topics, while Tatsuya and Miyuki broached nothing on their own. It was clear that Honoka and Shizuku were delicately avoiding subjects related to the Yotsuba family.

After Tatsuya and Miyuki returned their bento boxes to their carrying bag, and Honoka and Shizuku slipped their lunch trays into the dining cabinet's return slot, Miyuki prepared tea for the four of them, and it was only then that the mood changed.

"Miyuki—"

Honoka suddenly stood and spoke, her voice and expression both stiff with nerves.

"Yes?" Miyuki's smile disappeared, and she looked up at Honoka with a serious face.

From the side, Shizuku watched them both carefully. Tatsuya, too, quietly observed.

"Well... The thing is... I..." Honoka desperately wrung the words out of herself.

Miyuki waited, her eyes not straying from Honoka for even a moment.

"I-I'm not giving up!"

Miyuki, Tatsuya, and Shizuku all looked at Honoka—to see her intentions and to measure her determination.

"I'm not giving up on Tatsuya!" Honoka finished, not faltering despite the heavy gazes upon her.

"I can't let you have him," replied Miyuki without missing a beat. She then gracefully stood and extended her right hand to Honoka, as though offering a handshake.

"Losing isn't an option for me." Honoka took Miyuki's hand, her smile brimming with competitive spirit.

Miyuki also smiled. That said, it was too sharp, too determined an expression to be called pleasant.

Tatsuya tried to force the faintest of smiles onto his face but couldn't even manage that. Two girls had just declared themselves rivals for his affections. Unsurprisingly, he had no idea what kind of expression he was supposed to have.

Then there was Shizuku, who was even more stone-faced than usual. Well, normally she was merely hard to rouse, but she was far from expressionless. However, in this particular moment, she was deliberately maintaining a neutral expression.

The truth was that even now, she wanted Honoka to give up on Tatsuya as soon as possible. But Honoka had chosen to compete with

Miyuki for Tatsuya's heart. Shizuku knew a brutally thorny path lay ahead of her friend, and she was desperately trying to keep that knowledge from showing on her face.

The student council meeting held after classes were over for the day had a happy, cheerful atmosphere for the first time in quite a while. Both Izumi and Minami noticed the change, but neither girl was the type to pry. Their relief at the oppressive mood lifting was nonetheless obvious in their faces and demeanor.

But not everyone was so tactful—as one might expect in a room full of high school students.

It was near the school's closing time when Kasumi came up the stairs to the student council room and whispered, "Hey, Izumi. Does the mood here seem, I dunno, different somehow?" Though her voice was hushed, it was still somehow very audible.

"Does it? I don't know—it *seems the same to me*," replied Izumi with a pleasantly calm expression, which made it strangely hard to argue with her.

Kasumi realized she'd somehow said something to make Izumi angry, and despite not really knowing what was going on, she nodded and backed off. "Huh? Uh... Oh, okay."

"What's up with the mood in here?"

Mikihiko, having also just come up from the discipline committee room, had a reaction that was a bit less problematic than hers.

"What mood?" Tatsuya asked him.

"Ah, it's nothing," he answered—in the same way he would have before winter break and exactly the way he hadn't been the past week.

Mikihiko and Erika must've been nudged to shape up at the same time, Tatsuya mused, but of course he didn't say so aloud. He couldn't help the slight smirk that came unbidden, though.

"What's up, Tatsuya? Something good happen?"

"Maybe. Just a small thing, though." It *was* a small thing—but also an unmistakably good development. Both for Miyuki and for himself, Tatsuya concluded, then switched his attention elsewhere. "Anyway, let me see today's report."

"Here you go. No particular problems on campus."

Tatsuya glanced over the sheet of e-paper Mikihiko handed him, then input the student council's signature on it via a hardware key.

"Was there some kind of trouble off campus?" Tatsuya asked as he returned the paper to Mikihiko. His interest had been piqued by the other boy's careful specification of *on campus*.

"Yes… There's been an increase in incidents of students being surreptitiously photographed and followed."

"Stalkers?" To Tatsuya's dismay, this was the first he'd heard of it. His hands had been so full with his own problems recently that his attention had been focused on his immediate vicinity and no further.

"It's not that simple—apparently they're from a humanist group."

"You're saying an anti-magician group is targeting the students of our school?"

Tatsuya's eyes gained a sharp intensity.

Miyuki and Honoka, who had been chatting amiably as they prepared to head home, also stopped and looked to Mikihiko.

"Apparently, there haven't been any actual assaults on students. But we have had a few start to come forward with reports of verbal abuse."

"Minami," Miyuki called, sitting back down in the student council president's seat.

"Yes, president." Minami stood and began to approach, but Miyuki stopped her with a look.

"Have the incidents the disciplinary committee chief raised been acknowledged in the student council?"

"One moment please," Minami replied, flipping the switch on the desktop terminal she'd already powered down. Unlike the appliances common in the early part of the century, its boot time was close to zero, and the search screen was soon ready on the display.

Minami input the search terms and read out the results. "Twenty-four students have reported a total of thirty-eight incidents. In each case, they were reported to law enforcement, but no concrete response was recorded."

"They're just ignoring it?!" Honoka cried out in disbelief.

"It's hard to take action against just verbal abuse," Shizuku sighed.

"Setting the covert photography aside, it's also hard to prove that we're being followed," Mikihiko added, frustrated.

Tangible enemies, like the ones they'd faced in the Yokohama Incident, could be fought back and beaten. But this nebulous aggression whose perpetrators were indistinguishable from law-abiding citizens left no opportunity for retaliation. If they used force against these offenders, they'd become the villains. And they couldn't even be certain who their enemy was.

"We should issue a warning to the entire student body. In addition to warning them of the possibility of assault, we need to caution them against overreaction or else we'll be the real criminals," Tatsuya agreed.

"Understood. I'll see to it immediately," Miyuki replied.

It was Saturday, January 19, the weekend after the second week of the new term.

The morning classes had concluded, and the rest of the school day would be devoted to extracurricular and student committee activities.

Kasumi and Izumi Saegusa headed to the dining hall to replenish their energy before said activities began. Izumi had wanted to have lunch with Miyuki in the student council room but found herself unable to refuse Kasumi's spur-of-the-moment suggestion: "Hey, let's have lunch together for once."

Both Kasumi and Izumi were quite well-liked among the juniors and seniors, but that was doubly true for the freshmen. Neither of them was particularly nurturing, so no Kasumi Army nor Izumi Royal Guard had formed, but in staying out of any cliquish infighting, they had become broadly adored. This was in marked contrast to the Shippou Group that had formed around Takuma, thanks to his assiduous mentoring.

Since they didn't have a set group of admirers, it wasn't hard for them to keep to themselves. Even so, they quickly accumulated a ring of lunch tray–holding freshmen around them.

It was a particular feature of Kasumi and Izumi that the students who approached them were predominantly girls. This wasn't a Miyuki-type situation, where the boys were too intimidated to approach them, but rather attributable to their mascot-like status among the girls.

And so, despite the many students surrounding them, not a single one interrupted their conversation, so the two were able to speak freely to each other in between slurps of their soba and tempura lunch.

Izumi ate as fastidiously as her image would suggest, but Kasumi, too, had good table manners, breaking the chunks of tempura into bite-size pieces and eating them neatly. Since neither girl was the type to talk while chewing, the conversation proceeded rather slowly. The gentle, pleasant ambience of their lunch certainly made it difficult to guess at what the pair's conversation was.

"The school certainly has been gloomy the last two or three days."

"You mean the rumors going around about Miyuki and Tatsuya? I am getting rather tired of this sordid fuss that everyone seems determined to continue with."

"…Um, what does *sordid* mean?"

"Dirty or improper."

"Oh, so you want people to get their minds out of the gutter and to mind their own business, basically."

"To put it simply, yes."

"Why didn't you just say that?"

"I don't want to cast aspersions on our upperclassmen like that. I'd generally like to believe the students of this school are proper ladies and gentlemen."

"Seems like the same thing to me. If anything, the way you said it is nastier, Izumi."

"Not at all, Kasumi. I don't think everyone's nature is inherently dirty and low—I simply think the circumstances have temporarily made people inappropriately curious," Izumi replied with a pious expression, reaching for the small bowl on her lunch tray. (Incidentally, the lunches at First High came in large, medium, and small sizes.)

"I don't think you can necessarily hide your real feelings behind fancy vocabulary, though," Kasumi muttered as her sister's attention turned to focus on the bowl. Kasumi knew her younger twin well enough to know that if they didn't blow off steam regularly like this, conversations with Izumi would become intolerably tense.

But apparently, Kasumi had jumped the gun just slightly.

"Did you say something, Kasumi?" Izumi sniped as she put her chopsticks to the small bowl and looked up.

"Nothing at all," Kasumi replied, likewise reaching for her own bowl.

Kasumi slurped her noodles with a bit more gusto than her sister. Izumi furrowed her brow at her elder twin, then began to move her own chopsticks.

Having succeeded in using table manners to deflect the conversation, Kasumi put her bowl down and resumed talking as though nothing had happened. "By the way, what's the mood like in the student council room? It looked pretty peaceful from the small glimpse I got, but…"

"They're only a year older than us, but everybody seems to be acting like adults, I believe," Izumi answered in a tone that was not entirely complimentary. "Honoka Mitsui in particular seems to have quite a few feelings on the matter…but she's been cheerful and pleasant to both Miyuki and Tatsuya, which is to her credit."

"Huh… Well, I guess the president and Tatsuya have kept the lovey-dovey stuff to a minimum, so they're trying to be conscientious anyway."

Izumi scowled at the term *lovey-dovey*, but there was nothing incorrect about Kasumi's statement, so she didn't quibble. "I'm quite certain that no matter how close the friendship, no human relationship can go well without mutual conscientiousness and respect."

"So you're saying that good manners are important even with close friends?"

"Certainly. To say nothing of people who aren't even particularly close but still amuse themselves with irresponsible rumors—and since there are more people like that than there are conscientious friends, one can hardly help the mood turning sour."

Izumi paused there.

"But that's just common sense," she added, as though she'd suddenly remembered as much.

The many classmates listening intently to Kasumi and Izumi's conversation all looked shamefully down in unison.

Around the same time, the dining hall at the Magic University was bustling with students.

Among them was a visiting student from the Academy of Defense's Special Warfare Research Department. She was one of two female students who sat across from each other, a magic officer in training at the Academy of Defense. Not that anyone would know from looking at her—she looked not just like an average student at the Magic University but indeed any female student at any ordinary college.

"Geez, Mari! You don't have to laugh *that* much!"

"Sorry, sorry! It's just, Mayumi, you and *him*...?"

The visiting student was Mari Watanabe, a former head of the First High disciplinary committee, and her shoulders shook with mirth even as she apologized. Opposite her was a former First High student council president, Mayumi Saegusa, red-faced and glaring.

Mayumi's flush was clearly more from embarrassment than from anger. There was nothing intimidating at all about the tears welling up in the corners of her eyes. "Stop!"

"I'm sorry, really." Mari only managed to contain her laughter when Mayumi turned her back on her to sulk. "It's just...the head of your family making you and Tatsuya get married—"

"It's not a marriage! It's just an engagement!" Mayumi snapped, folding her arms.

Privately, Mari didn't see what the difference was, but she kept that observation to herself. "So why is anybody talking about having you and Tatsuya getting engaged anyway?"

The Magic University's schedule was more flexible than the Academy of Defense's, but that didn't mean that students had unlimited time for lunch, so Mari tried to move the conversation along.

"Well, you know about the big controversy, right?"

It had been Mayumi who'd brought the topic up. She'd wanted to complain about it. She turned back around to face Mari, being perfectly aware herself that further sulking was just a waste of time.

"The Yotsuba thing? I dunno—it was unexpected for sure, but at the same time I can kind of see it. I was surprised, though."

Describing the news as unexpected but somehow not unexpected sounded contradictory, but Mayumi didn't object to the observation because she'd had the same reaction Mari did.

"How much do you know, Mari?"

"How much? I mean...that the Shiba siblings are actually cousins who are both directly related to the Yotsuba family, that Miyuki Shiba was named as the successor to Yotsuba family leadership, and that she and Tatsuya Shiba are now engaged. What, is there more?" asked Mari suspiciously.

Mayumi closed her eyes and nodded. "So that really *is* all that's been made public. It turns out there's more to the story." Mayumi leaned forward over the table, and Mari mirrored the movement. "The day after the announcement of Tatsuya and Miyuki's engagement went out, the Ichijou family lodged a formal protest."

"A protest?" asked Mari, with an expression that said *I didn't know you could do that.*

Mayumi smiled wryly. "Yes, on the grounds that marriage between two closely related people may harm an important national asset—our magicians' genetic potential."

"*Asset*? How...?" Mari looked appalled. While the Ten Master Clans weren't generally uncomfortable with this way of thinking, this would have been a very odd phrasing indeed among the Hundred Families and magicians further outside the influential core.

And Mari's discomfort was quite justified—reasonable, even. In this context, *asset* was synonymous with *property*. Calling genes *assets* was not far from defining magicians like Mari and Mayumi as livestock. One wrong step could lead to a dangerous political ideology where genes were valued over individuals.

"I gotta say, this is one thing I really don't like about the Ten Master Clans," said Mari.

"I don't like it, either, but in this case, it's for a good cause. But that doesn't mean I'm happy about something as personal as my engagement being used for convenience."

"Is there more than that?"

Mayumi sighed as the conversation approached its crux. "So the Ichijou family objected on the grounds of marriage between close relatives and simultaneously proposed an engagement between their oldest son, Masaki, and Miyuki."

"Well, that's...sort of annoying and thoughtless..." Mari trailed off.

Mayumi's shoulders slumped. "Yeah, but I do think an engagement between Masaki and Miyuki is still more desirable than one between her and Tatsuya. Setting aside whatever their personal feelings are, that is."

"So it'd be a political marriage that would make the magic world happy." It struck Mari more like a mating of thoroughbred horses than a political marriage, but even she hesitated to say that out loud.

"Yes, but…it wouldn't be only for the families' benefit, I don't think. I mean, Masaki's the oldest son, so ordinarily he would be in the position of bringing his wife into the household." Mayumi's gaze shifted around awkwardly; she was obviously uncomfortable. "I think another reason the Ichijou family took such a forceful approach is that Masaki does have feelings for Miyuki."

"…Oh-ho." Mayumi grinned, finally catching on to Mari's awkward expression. "So that's how it is. Your father's trying to get you engaged to Tatsuya because you *like* him, eh?"

"No!" Mayumi's face was bright red as she slammed her palms down onto the table. If there hadn't been an acoustic isolation field in place, the sudden noise was definitely loud enough to have drawn the attention of others in the dining hall. "That scheming old bastard has the wrong idea about me! And he's just using me to harass the Yotsuba family!"

"*Oh?*"

"What's with that insinuating expression on your face?! This is a real problem for me!"

"So you *don't* want it?"

Mayumi fell silent at the pointed question. Mari's lip curled into an impish smile.

Realizing that she was in danger of confirming her friend's suspicions, Mayumi forced her frozen tongue into motion. "It's not that I'm against it… I just can't look at Tatsuya that way. It's impossible imagining being engaged to him."

"Why's that?" Mari instantly pressed the attack.

"Why? I mean..."

"Sure, if he's *just* Tatsuya Shiba, he wouldn't be a match for Mayumi Saegusa from *the* Saegusa family. But if he's a direct member of the Yotsuba family, that's a different story. As a potential son-in-law for the Saegusa family, he's got both the blood and the talent."

"He's two years younger than me!"

"I don't think a two-year age gap is that big of a deal. And anyway, does he even seem younger than you? If I were looking at the two of you side by side, I'd guess you were the younger one."

"H-how dare you! In that case, there's not much difference between him and you, either!"

"Uh, exactly what part of me looks younger than Tatsuya?!"

"You were always cozying up to him for help! *Ooh, I can't finish this, Ooh, the terminal's messed up, Ooh, I haven't finished writing this report.* Maybe *you're* the one with feelings for Tatsuya!"

"Excuse me, I have Shuu!"

"That doesn't have anything to do with whether you do or don't like Tatsuya, does it?"

Mayumi and Mari glared at each other, then both suddenly looked away.

Both of their faces were red. Normally this would have been the moment when they each summoned a smile and changed the subject to put the childish argument behind them. But this time, that didn't happen.

Mari was the one who'd lost her temper at Mayumi's escalation, but she soon regained a serious, stern demeanor. As she turned her gaze back to Mayumi, there was no trace of smile.

"Mayumi, what is it you really want to do?"

Mayumi flinched at Mari's shockingly serious tone. "Wh-what kind of question is that?"

Mari fixed her friend with a stern gaze. There was nothing remotely resembling a joke to be found in Mari's face. "It's not good for Tatsuya's sister, but it doesn't seem to me like there's any downside to this prospect for you."

"What're you talking about? I don't even like Tatsuya—"

"Just shut up and listen," Mari said sharply. "I know perfectly well why you've never had a boyfriend. I also know that you never pursued any sort of relationship with the oldest sons of the Juumonji and Itsuwa families because you wanted to push back a tiny bit at having your future decided for you."

Mayumi made no refutation of Mari's statement, but it wasn't because Mari had hit the bull's-eye—Mayumi wanted to let the other woman finish her point.

"You were always saying how you couldn't see Juumonji as a romantic partner, right? But isn't that because from the very beginning, you couldn't help being aware of him as exactly that? More than just being your classmate, he was a fellow member of one of the Ten Master Clans. So you saw him not from the point of view of Mayumi the high school student but as Miss Saegusa, the eldest daughter of the Saegusa family."

Mayumi said nothing. She simply listened to Mari, her face an expressionless mask.

"Whether he was attractive as a boy didn't matter—it was about whether he was suitable as a member of one of the Ten Master Clans. Romantic feelings are never going to grow from seeing someone like that. Even if you grew to respect him, you'd never love him."

Mari continued, disregarding Mayumi's unresponsiveness.

"But Tatsuya was different. When you met him, he was just a younger kid at school, and you got to know him and like him, and then only later found out he was part of a major clan. I personally think that your admiration for him is really just attraction, but I won't insist on that. I do know that you at least like him as a person. Am I wrong?"

"You're not wrong. I don't believe my regard for Tatsuya is romantic, but the rest of what you said is more or less right."

Mari nodded at Mayumi's brief answer. "This is the first time you, the eldest daughter of the Saegusa family, have been allowed to date someone you even *like*."

"Yes, that's correct."

"Okay, so—what do you want to do? No, that's a bad way to put it. Mayumi—"

"What?"

"Do you want to do nothing and simply wait and see? Or do you want to do something?"

"I don't like just waiting. But are you saying there's something I *can* do?"

"This is where I'd normally tell you to figure it out yourself, but… hmm. I don't know—you do have the option of trying to figure out exactly how you feel about Tatsuya."

Mayumi started to say *I already know that* but stopped herself. "What would be the point of that?"

"If you knew for certain that you had romantic feelings for Tatsuya, then your interests and your father's would be aligned. You could pretend that he was using you, while in fact you'd be the one using him."

"Me, using that sly, old bastard? I admit the idea is appealing." Mayumi felt a sinister smirk begin to form on her face, but she quickly suppressed it. "Wait, how am I supposed to be certain about something like that?"

"Well, you could just try going out with him, right?"

"Go out with somebody I don't even like?" As she said this, Mayumi realized her logic had become comically circular, so she walked it back and tried again. "Or I mean, someone I don't know whether I like or not?"

"That wouldn't be weird, right? People say stuff like that all the time—*Let's start as friends*."

"No, that's the kind of thing you say to someone you don't already know. It'd be really awkward for me and Tatsuya to *start as friends*. For starters, what if I'm wrong? I split up an engagement and then say, *Whoops, sorry, I'm not into you after all*? That'd be unacceptable!"

"You think?"

"Obviously!"

"Huh… Well, I guess in that case you'll just have to date him without his sister finding out."

"What? Why?!"

"Do you want to find out how you feel about Tatsuya or not?"

"No, that's what I've been saying this whole time!"

"Okay, so why are you coming to me for advice?"

Mayumi's expression froze.

"Lately all you do is complain to me about the arranged marriage meetings you have to suffer through. So maybe this is the first time someone who's already engaged has come up, but that's not the only reason you're not just letting it play out, is it? If it were really that clear to you, all you'd have to do is say you refuse to consider anyone who's already engaged."

"…I tried that. The old man just keeps pushing."

"Probably because he sees right through you. The truth is, you don't hate the idea."

"…"

"Mayumi, as long as you don't know what you really want, you're just going to keep getting swept along by your circumstances."

"That's easy for you to say…" Mayumi was completely at a loss. If she were pushed any further, she'd probably burst into tears.

Mari glanced conspicuously at her military chronograph. "—My time's up. Mayumi, make sure to think this through, okay?"

"Yeah… Thanks, Mari."

As Mari stood to leave, Mayumi rose sluggishly to her feet, too.

Upon returning home from school, Tatsuya frowned at a piece of mail from an unusual recipient. It wasn't electronic mail, strictly speaking, but rather a direct message on the message board system used by First High students and alumni.

The sender was Mari.

Tatsuya wondered if she'd sent it to the wrong person, but there was no way to determine that without opening the message. He briefly considered using a hack to inspect the contents without triggering the message's read receipt but decided that would be more trouble than it was worth. If he were certain he wasn't going to encounter Mari afterward, he wouldn't have hesitated, but there was no guarantee of that.

Keenly aware that this was likely going to lead to trouble, Tatsuya opened the message.

The first thing he saw was that he was indeed the intended recipient.

The message began with a simple, seasonally appropriate greeting. It then included recent events in Mari's life and an inquiry as to Tatsuya's well-being—all in all, it was an unusually formal piece of personal correspondence. Perhaps the result of officer candidate school.

The letter's actual point was a simple matter.

She wanted to meet tomorrow evening.

Private correspondence needed to be kept private—but perhaps this was an exception. He couldn't very well meet another girl alone without telling his fiancée.

Before replying to the message, he went and knocked at his sister's bedroom door.

"Mari Watanabe said she wants to meet with you?" Miyuki looked at Tatsuya with a very dubious expression. He'd supposed that a little bit of concern would be unavoidable but found it surprising at how little Miyuki seemed to trust him.

"I was rather bewildered myself at the sudden invitation," Tatsuya said, trying to emphasize the casual innocence of the situation. "We just saw her not long ago at the graduation ceremony, after all."

"I wonder what she wants, then."

Miyuki did not suspect Tatsuya of anything; she was suspicious of Mari's possible motives.

Tatsuya was a very desirable man (Miyuki thought). She knew Mari had a boyfriend, but it was entirely plausible (to Miyuki) that Mari would consider it sport to pursue an affair with Tatsuya anyway.

"I doubt she's angling for an affair," said Tatsuya bluntly, as though he'd seen right through Miyuki's wild imaginings.

Miyuki's face immediately turned red.

Tatsuya continued, pretending not to notice, "Watanabe's got a fine boyfriend in Naotsugu Chiba, after all."

"…Well, perhaps they had a fight," Miyuki shot back, pretending at anger to hide her embarrassment.

"If she wanted someone to complain to, I'm sure she'd go to Saegusa." Tatsuya smiled at her transparency, only to have his face turn serious. "…Actually, probably the other way around," he murmured.

"The other way around? You mean, Saegusa complaining to Watanabe?"

Tatsuya nodded. "This wouldn't just be limited to Watanabe. Any First High alum wanting to talk to us now has got to have something to do with our family situation."

"I…suppose you're right." Miyuki's immediate reaction was annoyance at the way some people ignored things like timing and circumstances and just imposed on other people however was most convenient for them. But she understood that such people were the minority and the exception to the rule and that, in this case, there was no way of knowing which it was.

"We're ignoring the exceptions where there's no way of knowing, okay?" Again, Tatsuya saw right through his sister.

"…"

Again, Miyuki's fair skin flushed.

While she looked down abashedly, Tatsuya continued his analysis: "If we're anticipating actions taken in response to the Yotsuba announcement, they're most likely to come from others in the Ten Master Clans. It's quite plausible that Saegusa is caught up in whatever the Saegusa family head is planning. Those plans probably upset Saegusa, and given her and Watanabe's relationship, it's also likely that she then went to Watanabe for advice."

"Don't tell me—!" cried Miyuki, her face still slightly red. She seemed extremely distressed.

Tatsuya paused his deduction, not understanding why Miyuki was so flustered. "What's got you so upset?"

"You...you don't suppose the Saegusa family is trying to get her engaged to you, do you?"

Miyuki's notion took Tatsuya by surprise. It was easy to see why the possibility made her uneasy.

"...I don't know, that seems like a bit of a leap to me."

It wasn't impossible to imagine. But to Tatsuya's mind, it was merely a very small probability, and it seemed very far from a realistic concern. Given what he knew of Mayumi, it was hard to imagine her contenting herself with being a pawn in a strategic marriage.

"I wonder..." Miyuki herself didn't think Mayumi would easily let herself be controlled by her parents. But if Mayumi had feelings for Tatsuya—that was a different story. "No, you're right." Miyuki nodded, banishing the worries from her mind. "So what will you do about Watanabe's invitation?"

"Well, I can't ignore it. And I would like to know why she went to the trouble," he replied, trying to avoid stirring up his sister's feelings further.

At 5:55 PM the next day, Tatsuya went to a café near the Academy of Defense's Special Warfare Research Department (SWRD) campus.

SWRD's curriculum was devoted to the use of magicians in the military and the training of magicians as military officers. It shared considerable research efforts with the Magic University, so its facilities had been built close to the university.

SWRD students were exempted from dorm living, but Mari had still proposed a meeting location near campus, as she had drills to attend even on Sunday.

Tatsuya had arrived at the designated spot five minutes early. At 5:59 PM, Mari appeared.

"Hey, Tatsuya, sorry if I made you wait. It's been a while, huh?"

"It has."

Mari removed her high-collared coat, revealing a pantsuit that wouldn't have been out of place in a corporate or government office. If she'd come directly from the Academy of Defense, she would have been in uniform. "I rent a room close to here," she explained, noticing Tatsuya's glance at her clothing—which meant that she had picked the café not because it was close to school but because it was close to where she lived. "But I did have drills today, just so you know! I'm sorry to ask you to meet me at such an odd hour."

"It's fine. What is this about?" Tatsuya didn't mean to be short with her, but as she had mentioned, it was rather late for a man and woman to be meeting each other alone. Given the location, it was likely that other Academy of Defense students frequented this place. Tatsuya wanted to get this meeting over with as quickly as possible in order to minimize the chance of misunderstandings.

"...I see your point. We've both got class tomorrow, so let's save the small talk for another time," Mari offered, ordering a hot coffee via the table's built-in terminal. "But I don't want to get interrupted, so hang on for just a second."

As stated, Mari was silent until her coffee arrived. She seemed to be collecting her thoughts for what she was about to discuss.

Perhaps fortunately, this café was not a so-called traditional establishment. Less than a minute later, there was a chime from the tabletop terminal. When Mari returned from the counter with her order, she squared herself before Tatsuya, then suddenly leaned toward him.

"Tatsuya, how do you feel about Mayumi?" she whispered.

Tatsuya answered with equal abruptness: "I think she's an excellent magician. She lacks for neither talent nor experience. As a person, she handles both public and private matters most admirably, hence my favorable impression of her."

"...You know, I hate it when you're like that." Mari glowered. Tatsuya had understood perfectly well what she'd been asking, and his answer was a barefaced deflection.

Tatsuya met Mari's scowl evenly. He didn't even leave her time to reach for her drink before replying, "So why are you asking me a question like that?"

"I'll ask you again," Mari insisted in reply. "What do you think of Mayumi as a member of the opposite sex? Just tell me whether you like her or not."

"I don't believe that feelings toward the opposite sex are as simple as that."

"And yet, here I am asking you."

Tatsuya had no obligation to answer Mari's question. It seemed to him that there were more downsides than upsides to any possible answer he could give.

And yet, he answered anyway. Not because he'd been bullied into it but because he wanted to see what would happen.

"I like her."

"As a girl? In *that* way?"

"Yes."

"Huh. Okay..."

For Tatsuya, the emotion of attraction to the opposite sex was not a very weighty one. It was among the emotions within him that had been artificially limited and as such was merely something that could be *processed*. Any such attraction was insignificant compared to his love for Miyuki. But he had no obligation to tell Mari that.

"Is it a romantic feeling?"

"No. If anything, it is only for her as an object of sexual desire," said Tatsuya evenly.

Mari flushed. "O-oh, so you *do* have those kinds of feelings."

Tatsuya mused that Mari was quite wholesome, which was a bit unexpected. The taboo against premarital sex that dominated in the era notwithstanding, she'd been dating her boyfriend for quite some time.

Of course, not even Tatsuya was so insensitive as to blurt *that* out.

"Of course I do. Sexual desire is a fundamental component of a natural reproductive instinct."

It wasn't a lie. But there was a limit to the strength of his sexual urges, and they would never be strong enough to dictate his actions— such was the influence of his true mother Miya's reconstruction of his psyche. Thus, Mayumi being an object of sexual desire didn't mean he was at all inclined to pursue her. But he had no obligation to tell Mari this, either.

"Watanabe, what is it you're trying to accomplish by asking me how I feel about Saegusa?"

His conversation partner still hadn't recovered from her fluster, but by forcing the topic, he pulled her out of her embarrassment, and she composed herself. "Would you consider going out with Mayumi, Tatsuya?"

"…By *going out with*, I assume you mean in a romantic way? Do you not know about me and Miyuki?"

Mari felt herself flinch away at the cold retort, but she pressed on: "I know that you and your sister are actually cousins and that you've been engaged."

"So you ought to know perfectly well that there's no way I can date Saegusa." The temperature of Tatsuya's gaze dropped even further.

I thought temperature-control magic was his sister's specialty, Mari thought as she braced herself to stave off frostbite. She knew that if she fell unconscious she wasn't going to die of hypothermia, but somehow that felt like a real possibility.

"The Ichijou family is interfering with your engagement, isn't that right?"

"You're well-informed. Did you hear this from Saegusa?"

News of the Ichijou family's formal objection was still not widely known. While Tatsuya and Miyuki's engagement had been legally acknowledged—although obviously if the truth were to come out, that acknowledgment would no longer stand, and there would be criminal charges for the Yotsubas' falsification of public records—the Ichijou family's actions were nonetheless already making the announcement into something of a scandal among certain circles of magical society. Given all that, Tatsuya had not openly discussed the subject much.

"Yeah, I did. And by the way, Mayumi's getting this, too. No— don't misunderstand me. I mean that Mayumi is being forced into the same position as the eldest Ichijou son is."

The iciness in Tatsuya's eyes vanished. It was replaced by a different chill, this time one that made Mari want to squirm in her seat.

"…Unbelievable."

Tatsuya's remark was aimed at the Saegusa family's calculation, but internally he was profoundly shocked at something else. Mayumi was being put forth as a possible engagement partner for Tatsuya: In other words, Miyuki's concern had been right on the money. Despite her youth, it seemed Miyuki's female intuition was a terrifying thing indeed.

"Yeah, that's what I thought, too," Mari casually replied.

Tatsuya met her remark with a sharp gaze. "Did you really? Do you really understand this?"

"Understand what?"

"That it won't be my reputation that suffers, it'll be Saegusa's."

Mari's eyes seemed to soften. "You're a nice guy."

"This is just basic consideration, in my view." Nothing was soft about Tatsuya's eyes.

"If Mayumi didn't have any particular feelings for you, I would've backed off. I would've told her there was no need for her to end up with the short end of the stick here. But she doesn't understand her own feelings."

So? Tatsuya's eyes asked.

"Mayumi doesn't know how she really feels about you. She doesn't understand what the nature of her affection for you is—she isn't even *trying* to understand. She won't face her feelings for you."

"And you don't imagine that that's because she understands her own position all too well?"

"Oh, she understands her position, all right. She can't just choose whoever she wants as her partner. Romance and marriage are unrelated. And if that's how it needs to be, then romance is meaningless. That's what she thinks."

"I think she's gotten ahead of herself, don't you? It's true that high-level magicians generally aren't allowed to remain single these days, but it's not like people aren't allowed to choose whom they marry."

"And what about you? What about your sister?"

Now it was Tatsuya's turn to fall silent.

Mari did not press the question of Tatsuya or Miyuki's feelings any further.

"I want her to experience love. Maybe it's overbearing or meddlesome of me, but I don't want her to make a perfectly informed surrender. You're a man, so maybe you won't understand."

"You're right. I don't understand."

"I figured. But try to understand this," Mari began, sincerity evident in her voice. "Mayumi feels affection for you. You might be the first and last man who can ever give her the experience of love."

It was clear she was only thinking of her close friend's feelings.

But Tatsuya shut her down. "You've gotten ahead of yourself, too."

"Tatsuya, you—!" Mari fumed, gaping.

Tatsuya's rebuttal stitched her mouth shut. "I may not know Saegusa as well as you do, but I don't think she's as weak as you think she is. She doesn't seem like the kind of woman to just abandon everything she thinks and believes to do whatever her parents tell her. I think she'll find love eventually, even if it's not me."

Tatsuya stood and looked down at the stunned, silent Mari.

"In any case, what you're asking remains impossible. I am Miyuki's fiancé."

The bill had already been take care of.

Tatsuya walked out of the café.

[4]

Raymond S. Clark was a high school junior in Berkeley, California, USNA. He'd been Shizuku's classmate when she studied abroad.

Unlike the magic high schools of Japan, the high school he attended had not been established specifically for magic education. Instead, magic studies and skills were offered as elective classes within a standard high school. But here, too, the number of schools with magic curriculums were limited, owing to a shortage of teachers. Because the number of applicants far exceeded the teaching capacity, schools had been forced to independently establish entrance examinations and selectively admit new students, and thus the school Raymond attended was for all practical purposes a magic high school like Japan's, dedicated to the education of magicians.

As such, it went without saying that Raymond was a magician-in-training. His abilities put him among the top of his class. He wasn't talented enough to get into the Stars, but he certainly had value elsewhere.

The USNA intelligence community referred to the secret society as the Seven Sages. In fact, it was not a single organization but rather seven individuals who had no contact with one another save for a single common point.

That was the hacking system known as Hlidskjalf, which was hidden within Echelon III, the global communications surveillance system funded by the USNA military. There were seven operators with access to the system. That was the common intersection the Seven Sages shared, and using Hlidskjalf, they could capture information from the world's communications networks with an efficiency and scale that far exceeded what Echelon III's legitimate operators were capable of.

Among the seven operators of Hlidskjalf, only one used the Seven Sages moniker. It was none other than Raymond himself, when on a whim he'd released information about an anti-governmental organization to the USNA authorities.

Today, Raymond was using Hlidskjalf again, awash in a sea of information. He liked knowing things. He liked investigating things, too, but simply stocking up on information without any particular goal in mind was something of a hobby to him. And Hlidskjalf was his very favorite toy.

That said, the nature of Hlidskjalf was still such that it required search terms. The system was made to answer questions, so it needed a question to work.

Points of light became letters describing the search terms. The Hlidskjalf terminal was a head-mounted VR display that used gestures and brain waves as input. A camera captured the user's movements and translated them into the operator's field of view. Using glowing characters projected in an imaginary space, the operator input search terms while a brain wave–assisted interface let them enter more specific commands.

Raymond was currently searching with the very broad term *USNA military misconduct*. Vast amounts of information were displayed in windows hanging in the virtual space around him. The more distant windows displayed only titles, while closer ones included more content. Some were text with diagrams, others were still images, and some were video. When he looked at a window it drew near, and when his gaze went elsewhere, it receded into the background. The space all around him, above and below, was filled with countless windows.

Raymond was a master of speed-reading and memorization. One after another, he rapidly internalized the contents of dozens of overlapping windows. But today he suddenly stopped. One particular window had caught his attention:

Older generation micro-missiles missing from weapons depot...?

It ought to have been a headline-making scandal. But sadly, it wasn't uncommon for obsolete weapons scheduled for disposal to go missing.

The missing missiles were man-portable air-defense systems (MANPADS) made for use by infantry soldiers and carried detonating warheads based on CL-20 (cyclotetramethylene tetranitramine) explosive. It was a weapon used during the 2020s and even well into the Global War Outbreak, but advancements in nanotechnology had led to breakthroughs in the power of explosive substances, so the obsolete missiles were now just gathering dust, awaiting disposal.

They'd still be plenty useful in an actual battle, though... I don't think this is a simple case of mismanagement.

Raymond licked his lips as he caught the scent of a major incident. He'd mastered speed-reading and memorization, but his greatest specialty was a curious ability to sniff out the distinctive odor of a serious mess.

Real-world incidents were the greatest show on earth, to Raymond. The bigger and more serious the incident, the more satisfying it was to discover and therefore the more fun.

He knew perfectly well that he was no superman. His magical talent was first-rate, but it would never reach the pinnacle his most accomplished peers were capable of. He would never be a magician powerful enough to influence world events. He would never be a globe-trotting superhero, no matter how much he wished for it.

Raymond had written off the possibility of that ever happening for him. Instead, he decided that if he could support the real heroes' activities even a little bit, it would allow him to get a taste of what adventuring with them would be like. And he'd let himself be entertained as the events played out on the world stage. Hlidskjalf made that possible.

It was as though Hlidskjalf had been made just for him.

I'll start by looking into the depot's management.

It wasn't as though a search for the location of the missing missiles was likely to return any hits. Humans were always involved. Someone had to be responsible for the diversion of weapons slated for disposal.

With practiced hands, Raymond began his search.

Before Raymond had noticed the disappearance of the obsolete missiles—to be specific, two days before—the incident had already sparked a commotion within the USNA military. The uproar wasn't confined to the weapons depot, either, as the Internal Affairs Office of the USNA Joint Chiefs of Staff's intelligence section had opened an investigation.

The reason Internal Affairs had opened the investigation rather than the military police was because of the suspicion that a terrorist group was involved, with the weapons having either been stolen by such a group or sold on the black market to one. If that were indeed the case, if the weapons' origin were to be revealed, it would be a huge scandal inviting international condemnation. The Ministry of Defense wanted to avoid that at all costs.

But by January 27, six days after the discovery of the missiles' disappearance, the investigation had progressed very little. At the office, despite it being a Sunday, the second-in-command of Internal Affairs, Colonel Balance, read the investigation's report as she harbored certain dark suspicions.

Namely, that there were far too few clues left behind.

She'd known from the beginning that the disappearance had to have happened with inside help. Weapons—even obsolete ones—couldn't simply be snatched from a military armory. But even if the unit leader responsible for securing the depot had been paid off, it shouldn't have been possible to take the missiles without leaving *any* trace.

There were multiple levels of checks involved when matériel entered or left the depot. In addition to all items being tracked with RFID tags, the doors were locked using biometric IDs and required two people to open them. There were multiple other security measures in place, both human and technological. And not a single one of them showed evidence of anything out of the ordinary.

What made Balance so uneasy was the question of why the disappearance had been noticed at all.

The discrepancy had been discovered during a physical inspection of the inventory. But since the theft had involved such complete falsification of the depot's data records, why hadn't the processing records also been tampered with? The missiles had been awaiting disposal. If they'd simply been marked as having been disposed of in the data, the discrepancy never would have been discovered at all. It felt to Balance as though whoever was responsible had wanted the fact of the theft—and *only* that—to be noticed.

But who and for what purpose? And who could pull off something like this in the first place?

There simply wasn't enough information to draw any solid conclusions. Balance knew as much but couldn't stop herself from worrying.

A chime announcing the arrival of an e-mail hauled Balance's mind up from the depths of her rumination. It was no ordinary message, either. It used encryption reserved for high-level intelligence officials.

With practiced, mechanical movements, Balance copied the encrypted message to a piece of specialized media that was unreadable to off-the-shelf, consumer computers, then fed it into an air-gapped decoder. This was to prevent against any potential leaks of the plaintext message. Once the message was decrypted and she saw the name of the sender, Balance's eyes went wide.

It read: "The Seven Sages."

The colonel's eyes turned frantic as she read the message, even forgetting to breathe. Only when she was done did she take several gasping breaths.

"Is this even allowed…?"

The anonymous tip stated that the assistant to the president's deputy chief of staff had been involved in the missiles' disappearance. It also explained the reasoning behind this. If what was written there was true, the release of disposal-scheduled weapons was only a small part of a huge plot, the scale of which vastly exceeded anything Balance would have imagined.

Balance reached for her visiphone, but her hand stopped short of touching the number pad.

She hesitated over whom to call, then shortly realized she had no idea.

If she didn't know who she could trust, then she didn't know who she should tell.

Angelina Sirius Shields, the commander of the Stars, the magician unit directly attached to the USNA Joint Chiefs of Staff, was enjoying a rare day off by shopping to her heart's content. She was out and about not as the strategic-class magician Angie Sirius, but rather as a seventeen-year-old girl named Lina.

The reason she had come all the way to Albuquerque instead of the nearer Roswell was because her shopping companion, Silvia Mercury First, call sign Silvie, had strongly insisted on the destination.

Ever since their tour of duty in Japan the previous year, the two often spent off-duty time together. Silvie regarded Lina as something of a troublesome little sister. From Silvie's perspective, Lina had a variety of deficiencies in her common sense as a woman, and Silvie was possessed by a powerful sense of duty not to let her go astray.

Today, Lina had again played the doll in the game of dress-up that was Silvie's approach to shopping. Fortunately, Lina herself had also enjoyed it. She hadn't been blessed with much fashion sense, but she did enjoy wearing nice clothes. Given her natural beauty, she'd probably never felt a pressing need to improve her fashion sense. The lack of someone she wanted to impress was the biggest thing that differentiated her from Miyuki on that count.

Nevertheless, Lina returned to her quarters at the base in high spirits as she carried her spoils of war. It had been a rejuvenating day off. She hadn't been mobilized as Sirius for a while, and the training that awaited her tomorrow would be intense. She was pleased at having had such a refreshing day.

However, her buoyant mood evaporated as soon as she opened the mail that had reached her quarters' terminal.

"A special encrypted message?!"

It wasn't particularly rare for her to receive messages related to her duties at her personal terminal. But this was the first time a message using the special encryption reserved only for Stars captains, staff headquarters' communication with those captains, and chief commanders had ever come to the terminal in her quarters.

Lina wondered if there was some kind of an emergency. After waiting for the decryption to finish with a mixture of impatience and nervousness, she looked at the message's plaintext and murmured, astonished, "The Seven Sages…?"

That was the sender's name.

For a moment, Lina wondered if it was a prank, but she soon dismissed the idea. No bored hacker would be able to use Stars-level encryption. And in any case, the Seven Sages moniker wasn't widely known outside of sections under the direct control of the Joint Chiefs of Staff.

Lina hastily started reading the message. At a glance, it seemed to contain the particulars of an incident that had nothing to do with her regular duties.

However, as she got closer to the end of the message, facts that were deeply relevant to her began to make their appearance.

"What?! The figure who masterminded the parasite incident?!"

Lina had been dispatched to Japan to identify the strategic-class magician responsible for the use of the Great Bomb (the USNA's term for Material Burst) off the southern tip of the Korean Peninsula. But when the desertion and subsequent escape into Japan of parasite-possessed members of the Stars was revealed, the order to eliminate them had come to Lina, the Stars high commander.

Lina had been told that the parasites' emergence was an accident. The incident had been purely accidental and, with the deaths of the individuals involved, was closed. But if the incident had been orchestrated by somebody, that person was also responsible for compelling Lina to kill her own people. It was their fault that on top of everything else, she'd been forced to act as an assassin.

This was not something she would ever forgive.

"The figure behind the parasite incident is planning to use stolen missiles to commit acts of terrorism in Japan?! This has got to be a joke, right?!" Lina yelled in spite of herself, upon reaching the end of the message.

This was information from an unknown source that couldn't be verified. There was no guarantee whatsoever that it was true.

USNA military profilers had concluded that the Seven Sages' criminality was motivated primarily by the sheer fun of it. Even if this message genuinely came from them, Lina was well aware that she might simply be caught up in some elaborate prank.

And yet, Lina believed the information was true.

The previous year, near the conclusion of the parasite incident, she'd been e-mailed intelligence from someone identifying themselves as one of the Seven Sages. Then, too, she'd had no reason to trust it. But she had.

Today, it was the same. There was no basis for verification. No reason to believe.

But being tricked, fooled, and made a laughingstock was better than ignoring the information, doing nothing, and living to regret her inaction.

If the intrigue detailed in the message was true and this scenario was playing out in reality, the USNA would end up deeply indebted to Japan. Relations between the two nations were already tense, and if USNA-made weapons were used for terrorist activities in Japan, the USNA would be inescapably suspected of aiding terrorism.

Given the relative power of Japan and the USNA, war was fairly unlikely. But that was only assuming conventional warfare. If the range of the strategic-class magic responsible for the Scorching Halloween could extend across the Pacific Ocean—which should have been impossible, to Lina's understanding as a strategic-class magician herself—the worst-case scenario could come to pass.

So Lina believed the message.

She had to prevent this terrorism. And not just stop it from happening but put an end to its mastermind by her own hand.

However, according to the message from the Seven Sages, Gide Hague—the mastermind—had already escaped the USNA and was heading for Japan. It was difficult for Lina to take action outside of her own country, let alone in Japan.

She decided to consult the only person she knew who could help her get to Japan.

The visiphone continued to ring as Virginia Balance reached for—and failed to touch—it.

But with effort, she relaxed her posture and calmly pressed the ANSWER CALL button.

There on the screen was Lina, wearing the dark purple uniform of the Stars. *"Colonel, my apologies for the interruption."*

Lina's uniform was meticulously neat, as though she'd just put it on, a thought which Balance found faintly amusing. "Major Sirius. Aren't you on leave today?"

Lina's face betrayed surprise. She wasn't directly under Colonel Balance's command, so it surprised her that the colonel would know or care about the specifics of her duty schedule. From Balance's perspective, however, it was obvious why any soldier above a certain rank attached directly to the Joint Chiefs of Staff would follow the movements of one of the strategic-class magicians known as the Thirteen Apostles, the USNA military's strongest magician, and the high commander of the Stars.

"Ah, sorry, not a relevant question. So what do you have for me?" Balance asked, slipping in an apology for opening with idle chatter.

"Ma'am. I've come with some information and a request for assistance," Lina began at the prompt.

"Continue."

"Yes, ma'am. While I was out on leave between 0900 and 1632 hours, I received intelligence in an encrypted message from someone calling themself the Seven Sages."

"As in *the* Seven Sages?" Balance asked with a perfect poker face, betraying none of the sudden concern she felt.

"That was the name in the message's sender field. I don't know if they're the real thing or not."

"I see," said Balance, nodding at the camera for Lina to continue.

"Presuming that the sender is who they say they are, the Seven Sages informed me of a terrorist plot to use stolen USNA weapons that had been slated for disposal. The target is Japan."

"What type of weapons?"

"MANPADS."

"...Major, do you actually believe that such a theft occurred?"

"I don't know the truth. But I have heard rumors that some weapons scheduled for disposal were stolen."

Balance sighed. Lina was thoroughly sequestered from the common soldier—if even a sheltered officer like her had heard the rumors, it meant that the lax military discipline surrounding the administration of weapon depots had become the rule rather than the exception.

"Colonel?" Lina's expression was uneasy, seemingly worried that she'd somehow upset Balance.

Balance herself realized as much—although for her part, it was a regrettable situation. "Ah, it's nothing. Please, continue."

"Ma'am, there wasn't any information about their concrete objectives, but I did get the name of the apparent mastermind: Gide Hague. A political refugee after the destruction of Dahan, his Chinese name is Gu Jie. His estimated age is somewhere between sixty and ninety. Black eyes, white hair, and fairly dark skin for someone of East Asian descent. There was special mention made that he might be a survivor of the Kunlun Institute."

"The Kunlun Institute? As in the magic research facility in Dahan that was wiped out by the Yotsuba?"

"I believe so, ma'am."

Balance momentarily wondered if they were actually planning retaliation against the Yotsuba specifically using portable missiles but then quickly dismissed the thought as absurd. If the Yotsuba clan could be harmed by anything like that, they wouldn't be so fearfully regarded as untouchable.

"Also," continued Lina as Balance turned the thought over in her mind, *"the message revealed Gide Hague as the figure behind the parasite incident."*

Balance's face registered the clarity of her understanding. "So that's the reason for your call."

Lina was unworried by the exposure of her primary motive. *"Colonel. Even if the intelligence that Gide Hague was behind the parasite incident is true, we don't know how deeply involved with it he was. But if he was even slightly responsible, I cannot overlook that. I will not be satisfied until I have had my reckoning with him."*

"Are you saying you want to go to Japan, Major Sirius?"

"Affirmative, Colonel."

Balance scowled as though she had a headache.

It was difficult for Lina to leave the country. Dispatching any magician abroad required careful consideration, but it was an order of magnitude more difficult when the individual in question was the strategic-class magician Sirius. One of the USNA's other strategic-class magicians, Laurent Barthes, was stationed in the British territory of Gibraltar, but he rarely left the base there. He was recalled home for any leave he took. Lina's mission to Japan the previous year was an exceptionally rare event.

Balance saw that Lina herself knew this, which was why she'd called. And Balance could also understand Lina's desire to either capture or liquidate Hague.

"...I can't give you an immediate answer. Give me a day, Major."

On the other side of the screen, Lina's eyes went wide. She had assumed there was a high possibility her request would be denied, so Balance's answer was unexpectedly promising.

"Ma'am! Thank you very much, Colonel."

Lina's salute was still on the visiphone's screen when Balance ended the call.

Meanwhile, Gide Hague, otherwise known as Gu Jie, was at sea.

Until recently, he had lived on the West Coast of the former United States, but he didn't have USNA citizenship.

Gu Jie's homeland was Dahan. A ruined nation. He'd been affiliated with the Kunlun Institute, Dahan's magic research and development facility. Upon the destruction of Dahan he'd received refugee status from the USNA government, so he was now stateless.

However, when Jie had first crossed over to North America, it was 2054, and the nation was still known as the United States of America. Dahan had fallen in February of 2064, and the destruction of the Kunlun Institute had come just a year before that.

Gu Jie hadn't left Dahan because of its ruin, nor even because the Kunlun Institute had been destroyed. Rather, he'd escaped from it.

The Kunlun Institute had existed before East Asia had split into Dahan and the Great Asian Alliance and was considered the main East Asian modern magic research facility.

But this was not precisely accurate.

While the Kunlun Institute was an East Asian research facility, it didn't only research modern magic. It conducted studies into both ancient and modern magic.

However, as in other nations, there was antagonism between the two sides.

Japan's Lab Nine had originally been established to put ancient magic techniques and expertise to use in the development of modern magic. It wasn't meant to be a facility for researching both ancient and modern magic as equals, and this had ultimately invited a revolt by the ancient magicians, and that antagonistic structure had been passed on even after the shuttering of Lab Nine.

This was even a problem in organizations where the primary position was thoroughly established. In research institutions dedicated to either, modern and ancient magicians fought bitterly over objectives, budgets, and personnel.

And at the Kunlun Institute, too, there were struggles for hegemony between the modern and ancient magicians.

The conflict continued even after Dahan took over the institute. In fact, conditions worsened and before long, the facility was near collapse. In the end, the modern magicians won the struggle, and the ancient magicians were expelled from the Kunlun Institute. This was in 2054.

It was then that Gu Jie, one of the ancient magicians, fled to the

United States with his apprentice Gongjin Zhou. There was originally no reason why Jie would have any grudge against either the Yotsuba clan or Japan's magicians more generally. As the ones who'd destroyed the Kunlun Institute in his place and eradicated the modern magician faction there, the Yotsuba clan was—or could have been—*the enemy of my enemy*, as far as Jie was concerned.

But after the destruction of Dahan, he settled on the Yotsuba clan and Japan's magical community in general as the target for his vengeance. There was no way for anyone to know what psychological process led to that decision, and by now, he himself may no longer have remembered.

Was it patriotism?

Was it resentment over having the proper objects of his revenge stolen from him?

Did he simply need something to maintain control over his followers?

What was known was that Gu Jie had built a criminal network made up of refugees from Dahan and that he carefully steered its activities in order to gather power for his revenge. That was currently all that was certain about the man.

As Zhou had put it while he was still alive, Jie's long-hardened obsession had made him into nothing less than a vengeful ghost.

It wasn't a compulsion that came from rational thought and was thus not something that would stop because of a well-reasoned weighing of pros and cons. Upon losing Gongjin Zhou, his last follower and disciple, Gu Jie had finally decided to take matters directly into his own hands.

That said, he had little combat ability. He was a user of ancient magic, and the techniques he'd acquired were of no use in a direct confrontation. Zhou had been the one with the power to face down their enemies, as Jie himself freely admitted.

Gu Jie's specialties were creating magical tools using other people as components (as in Sorcery Boosters), changing humans into tools (as in Generators), and controlling dead bodies.

It was as though someone had condensed all the most ghoulish facets of magic into a single practitioner. Setting aside the ethical ramifications, he wasn't the kind of magician normally found fighting on the front lines. And in fact, before now, he'd always devoted himself to pulling the strings behind the scenes.

Gu Jie was now heading for Japan only because he'd been cornered into it.

Blanche, the international anti-magic political group that he'd supported, had found itself considerably weakened owing to mounting pressure and scrutiny from several countries. The international crime syndicate No-Head Dragon, whose boss he'd backed, had been destroyed in a joint operation between Japanese and USNA intelligence agencies (with the tacit approval of the Great Asian Alliance).

And he'd lost Gongjin Zhou, his agent in Japan. Zhou had been Jie's final pawn, the one person who'd been with him ever since their escape from Dahan forty years earlier. With his death, Jie had no choice left but to act personally.

Zhou had been killed in October of the previous year.

Jie had set out from the port of Los Angeles in the latter half of the following January.

The two-month gap was not because he was sitting on his hands or mourning the death of his disciple. It was the result of his careful planning to secure the most effective stage for his revenge. He would've preferred to exact his retribution immediately, but if he failed this time, there would not be another chance. He was certain of it.

He had no magic that gave him any options for attack. His techniques weren't useless, but he lacked the power to go up against a top-ranking magician. So his first order of business had to be the acquisition of weapons.

If Blanche or No-Head Dragon had been as powerful as they once had been, this would've required nothing more than a word from him—but now to assemble a respectable arsenal took him well over a month.

Simultaneously, he had to arrange for passage across the Pacific Ocean, which he also managed himself. More precisely, he accomplished this with a temporarily hired lackey he made into a disposable puppet, but since the puppet required carefully worded orders for every single task it performed, it was hardly less effort than if he'd simply done it himself. Then he'd loaded the puppet onto the boat so it couldn't be traced to him and disposed of it at sea.

Beneath the photovoltaic panels that covered the entire deck of the cargo ship, Gu Jie looked out over the ocean as the ship's captain approached him.

"Mr. Gu. We expect to arrive in Yokosuka Port tomorrow morning."

"So on schedule, then," said Jie in a steady voice that betrayed no exhaustion.

Gu Jie was currently ninety-seven years old, but he looked like a man in his fifties. His hair had gone completely white, but his unusually dark skin showed minimal wrinkles and no sagging or liver spots.

"Also, sir…about my compensation…"

"Yes, I'm aware. I'll perform the technique tomorrow morning before dawn, as I promised."

"Thank you, sir! Even after this voyage ends, you shall have my undying loyalty!"

Gu Jie nodded with a satisfied expression, but behind it, he contemptuously regarded the captain as a fool.

The captain's hoped-for compensation—it was a halt to aging and an extended life.

It was true that Jie had a magic technique that stopped the aging process. His own *external* appearance was the proof.

But even though that was an apparent guarantee of delaying the effects of age, it was no promise of lengthened life, much less anything as spurious as immortality.

Jie had developed the technique while at the Kunlun Institute, and it was the reason why ancient magicians had been expelled from that same institute.

As the powerful were wont to do, the leaders of Dahan sought perpetual youth. To that request, the modern magic faction of the Kunlun Institute answered that it was impossible, while the ancient magic faction assured them that it was possible. To the ancient magicians, who had fallen behind the modern faction in the pursuit of the Kunlun Institute's original goal of weapon development, this was their one chance to recover their status.

In the ancient magic group, it was Jie's whose magic was the most promising. This, of course, was his antiaging procedure.

It was the year 2049 when he used himself as an experimental subject for the technique.

In order to verify the procedure's safety, nine of his followers underwent the same procedure in 2050.

Five years later, in 2055, it was confirmed that Gu Jie had stopped aging. His followers likewise showed no sign of aging, and the magic was considered a viable path to perpetual youth and a lengthened life span.

But the technique had a catch. It was true that the antiaging procedure *appeared* to halt the aging process. But when used on someone without the particular aptitude for it, the subject would die within three to six months, as though the magic were consuming their very life force in the process of preserving youth.

No magic could remain in effect indefinitely. On that point, both modern and ancient magic agreed. The antiaging procedure relied upon the subject itself to continually recast the necessary magic.

The technique was made for ancient magicians who possessed the abilities of Taoist immortals.

What would become of a magician who continued to use magic they had no capacity for?

What would become of a non-magician forced to use magic?

The antiaging procedure provided one answer to those questions.

When the leaders of Dahan offered the fruits of the immortality project to their family members, the resulting access to more human experimental subjects confirmed to Gu Jie the incompleteness of his technique.

The result was the expulsion of the ancient magic group.

Quickly realizing his failure, Gu Jie fled with his followers to the United States.

Twenty years later, he knew that the technique he'd invented also failed to extend life. His followers' deaths proved it.

In the end, what he'd created was a technique that merely halted the superficial outer effects of aging. The reason Gu Jie himself had lived so long was merely due to his normal, natural longevity.

And it was that incomplete magic that the cargo ship captain wanted.

Gu Jie found this comical.

It was none other than Jie himself who'd told the captain about the antiaging magic. To make the man his pawn, Jie had explained there was a secret technique that would keep you young until you died, and in exchange for the captain's cooperation, Jie would cast it on him.

He wasn't lying. The cargo ship's captain would enjoy his current youth until the day he died. That day would probably come within six months.

And Jie himself did not have much time left. Of that, he was very aware.

"I'll be very busy starting tomorrow," he murmured.

"I can be of use to you even after we've docked. You have only to say the word, sir!" replied the captain proudly, ignorant of what his passenger's true intentions were.

Balance had told Lina to let her think the matter over for a day but had taken quick action.

She'd made arrangements for an early excursion from her office, leaving the next morning. The destination: Stars headquarters on the outskirts of Roswell, New Mexico.

Balance quickly wrapped up all the next day's most urgent paperwork and then went home, where she sent an e-mail using the encryption device hidden there. The unit had been given to her by Ayako Kuroba, and the e-mail she sent was to Maya Yotsuba. In it, she related the report largely as Lina had given it—that there was a terrorist plot brewing to use stolen portable missile launches in Japan, and that its mastermind, Gide Hague, was likely a survivor of the Kunlun Institute.

Balance didn't include the fact that the source for this intelligence wasn't actually Lina herself. It concerned a scandal within the USNA government, after all. Balance had secured an alliance with the Yotsuba family, but that didn't mean she trusted them completely, and she was certain they felt the same way. She had no compunctions about appealing to a colleague, but she couldn't risk endangering national relations.

As Balance was eating dinner, she received a reply from Maya thanking her for the information. This wasn't particularly meaningful to Balance, but she also didn't mind. The purpose of the mail she'd sent was primarily to firmly establish that she was intent on meeting the obligations of their alliance.

Finally, she reconfirmed the schedule of the various Stars commanders, then headed for the showers.

It was Monday, January 28, at 8:00 AM Japan time, when Maya received the e-mail from Balance.

"Hayama, apparently a remnant from the Kunlun Institute is planning a terrorist attack right here in Japan."

"Good heavens, madam," said Hayama noncommittally. He of

course knew how Maya had been treated at the hands of the Kunlun Institute. Given Maya's feelings on the matter, it was only reasonable not to offer a more definitive reply, even if her voice in that moment wasn't particularly angry or embittered.

"Does this merit a *good heavens*? We're talking about a stray dog with no place to call home."

Maya's voice wasn't completely expressionless, though; she had donned a distinctly contemptuous demeanor.

"Madam, for there to be a survivor of the Kunlun Institute, this person would have had to elude your predecessor and *his* predecessor," said Hayama, chiding Maya for her hubris. "We have no idea what sort of unusual ability this person may possess. I strongly recommend caution."

"Oh, I'm perfectly aware," Maya muttered even as her lips were twisted in a cold smile. "But what do they think they can accomplish with a few missiles? Japan isn't some failed state. Walking around with a missile launcher is practically begging to be caught."

"During the Yokohama Incident, the guerrillas did in fact use portable missile launchers after they came out of hiding."

"That's because they had support from that disguised warship," Maya shot back reflexively only to quickly retract her objection. "...But no, it's true there's no way to guarantee we can prevent any and every possible terrorist act."

"Even a magician can be killed by a missile strike if they're caught off guard. And if terror is the goal, they don't even have to use the missiles as they are. The warheads could be removed and used as explosive devices. During the Global War Outbreak, such suicide attacks were seen all over the world."

Faced with such scenarios, Maya could not deny the need to act. "Fine. We'll search for Gide Hague or Gu Jie or whoever he is. But with the Master Clans Council quickly approaching, I doubt we'll be able to spare many people."

In early February 2097, the very next month, the impending

Master Clans Council awaited. In particular, the selection conference for the Ten Master Clans—an event that happened only once every four years—was scheduled on the council's second day.

This was a meeting that would decide the Ten Master Clans for the next four years. For the Twenty-Eight Families who were eligible for this status, this time of year was their last chance to assemble anything that would give them an edge in the selection conference. The selection itself was held by mutual vote of the Twenty-Eight Families, and while there wasn't open campaigning, there was constant fault-finding and glad-handing to garner support behind closed doors.

The Yotsuba family could not afford to ignore the privilege of being one of the Ten Master Clans, either. For the past four years—and before that—they had devoted considerable human resources to scrutinizing the negotiation materials they'd collected.

"Shall we share this information with the other Clans?"

Maya paused for a moment to consider the question of whether to seek the cooperation of the Ten Master Clans and the Eighteen Support Clans. She shook her head. "I don't want them prying into our source for the intel. But…go ahead and leak the rumor that a foreign terrorist planning violence against magicians has entered the country. Whoever wants to act on that is more than welcome to. Can you start by lunch?"

"Yes, madam. You may expect progress within two hours," Hayama said with a bow, referring to both the search for the terrorist and the manipulation of the rumor.

On January 28, at 9:00 AM local time, the cargo vessel carrying Gu Jie docked at the Port of Yokosuka.

Upon landfall, he immediately set about gathering the personnel he would need—but the arrangements had already been made before he'd arrived. Though he'd lost his pawns in No-Head Dragon, during his time as its puppet master Jie had cultivated considerable expertise in the broader criminal society. If one didn't care about quality, it wasn't hard to recruit people. No matter how prosperous a society, there were always some who fell through the cracks.

He had identified his target before making land. The location of the Master Clans Council was a secret except to its participants, but with the use of Hlidskjalf, discovering it was a simple matter.

Hlidskjalf, the super-hacking tool. Gu Jie wasn't in the habit of applying superlatives to things, but *super* was simply the only way to describe the system.

The scope of Hlidskjalf's information-gathering ability was the entire world. Jie knew he couldn't access anything that was strictly off-line, but in the modern era, the amount of useful information that had never been uploaded to a network was practically zero. Furthermore, Hlidskjalf could crack even the most hardened encryption. It even overturned and rendered moot the grand promise of quantum encryption systems that were, in principle, impossible to intercept without disturbing the decryption key.

Who had created such a system? Who had delivered to him the terminal that connected to it and for what purpose? Jie had been very suspicious at first. He'd performed searches of no particular value to himself in an attempt to flush out whatever sinister purpose lurked within the system.

The drawback was abruptly clear.

Hlidskjalf kept a record of all searches performed using the system. Other operators could freely view that record.

But crucially, nobody knew who had performed which search. All that was known was what had been searched *for*.

Jie had been disappointed. He'd imagined all along that whoever had given him access to the system would be able to see what he was searching for. None of the seven Hlidskjalf operators knew the others' real identities, but Jie wasn't (he thought) so naive as to consider that sufficient reason to trust them. The system administrator who'd sent him the terminal had to know who was searching for what. As long as Jie kept that fact in mind when he used the system, his search history being visible to the other operators couldn't be considered harmful.

His hesitation to use Hlidskjalf had vanished in an instant.

Of course, he was always aware that the system could be lying to him. He was careful to externally verify any information he found with it. Frequently, he couldn't corroborate things he'd learned and was thus unable to use the information. Even so, Hlidskjalf was a convenient and useful tool.

The problem currently facing him was that, having searched for the hotel where the Master Clans Council would be held, it was possible to infer from his search history that someone was planning to attack the council. Gu Jie did not underestimate the Ten Master Clans. If someone with a connection to the Clans—or someone who shared their interests—were a Hlidskjalf operator, they could set a trap for him at the council's meeting location. Naturally, he'd been as cautious as he always was when specifying his search terms, but just because things had gone smoothly thus far was no guarantee that they would continue to do so.

Taking all this into consideration, he'd gathered enough people to achieve his goal even if he was ambushed.

Gu Jie's goal was not the assassination of the heads of the Ten Master Clans. His plan was to *socially* bury the ones responsible for the destruction of the Kunlun Institute—the Yotsuba family.

As he watched the series of freight trucks carrying his many dolls toward Hakone set off, Gu Jie felt a dark pleasure well up within him and smiled. The raw materials for these dolls had come from the good, impoverished citizens of Yokosuka.

Lina was confused by the sudden cancellation of her drills but reported to the base commander's office as ordered.

Accompanying her was the commander of the Stars' First Unit, Benjamin Canopus. He was Lina's second-in-command, and she placed a great deal of trust in him.

"Ben, what do you think this is about?"

Canopus shook his head in response to Lina's question, which she'd posed in a voice tinged with uncertainty. "If I'm honest, I have no idea. We haven't broken anything recently, and I don't think there's anything else the brass can scold us for."

The Stars often destroyed things during training. Accessories, vehicles, training facilities—all sorts of things. Given the nature of combat training, this was unavoidable to some degree, but occasionally the Stars—particularly their commanders—went beyond what could be called *unavoidable*. Thus, Lina was frequently subjected to complaints from the base management.

"Y-yeah, you're right," said Lina in a small voice, trying to summon some courage. Canopus smiled encouragingly. He had a daughter only two years younger than Lina, so he couldn't help but be somewhat protective of her.

Meanwhile, unaware that she was being regarded so warmly, Lina balled up her hands into fists and nodded, trying to steel herself. The childish gesture only made Canopus's paternal feelings toward her stronger, though she herself had no idea this was happening right beside her.

Having successfully pushed her anxiety down, Lina assumed—she thought—a properly composed, soldierlike expression and knocked on the door of the base commander's office. A voice inside said, "Come in," and the door unlocked.

Lina opened the door, and she was so surprised at the unexpected figure that greeted her that she couldn't help but exclaim out loud, "Colonel Balance?!"

The base commander sat behind his desk and sitting next to him was Colonel Balance.

"Major, what are you doing? Come in," ordered the base commander, another colonel named Walker.

Lina hastily did so, standing in front of the desk. Canopus calmly joined her.

"At ease, Major Sirius, Major Canopus," said Walker to the two saluting officers who faced his desk.

"Sir!"

Lina and Canopus simultaneously stood at ease.

"Colonel Balance wants to have a word with you," Walker said, standing. "They're all yours, Colonel."

Balance took Walker's cue and also stood. "Thank you, Commander Walker. We'll only need the room for a moment."

Walker and Balance saluted each other, and Walker left the room.

Balance locked the door via remote control, then finally turned to face Lina. "Major Sirius, I imagine you know why I'm here. It's about what we discussed yesterday."

"Ma'am!" As Balance said, Lina had a hunch that this might involve the answer to the request she'd made the previous day.

"Unfortunately, Major, I can't grant your request." The answer was just what Lina had expected. "You're the high commander of Stars and a strategic-class magician. I can't send you abroad lightly."

It was reasoning that Lina had gotten used to hearing, but that didn't mean she could bring herself to agree with it. Last year, when she'd been dispatched to Japan, even though she ended up being the right person for the job, the initial mission had been well outside her specialty, and it made her feel like the personnel selection had been totally random.

The Stars would be the perfect unit to send to a friendly country to deal with a terrorist threat that her own country's misconduct had exposed it to. If nothing else, Lina was confident it was the right choice as she reflected back on her last trip to Japan—and all the more so because the mastermind seemed very likely to be a magician.

But Lina's frustration was neatly parried by Balance's next words.

"—That's the official reasoning. The brass are concerned that you're too sympathetic to Japan, Major. Some of them are even suspicious that you might defect."

Lina couldn't stop herself from objecting. "Wait just a minute! I've sworn loyalty to my country!"

"I know," said Balance, her tone sympathetic. "I don't doubt your loyalty, Major. But your Japanese ancestry and the fact that you're only seventeen are enough to inspire concern in others."

Lina was mortified. Physically, she looked entirely Anglo-Saxon, and she'd never been exposed to any sort of prejudice or racial discrimination before. But that held true only when discussing open bigotry, and the fact that behind the scenes such discrimination was indeed happening made her blood boil.

"I can only call it utter foolishness. But that doesn't mean you should give fools like that any sort of opening. Major, you are this nation's trump card."

Despite a fury that clouded her vision in red, Lina's training kept her rage from distracting her from her superior officer's words.

"I cannot dispatch you to Japan, Major Sirius. However, this also isn't a situation we can afford to ignore." Balance paused for a breath, then continued, putting some force into her voice. "As such, I will be sending Major Canopus to Japan. I trust that will be acceptable, Major Sirius?"

Lina tamped her frustration down and saluted. "…Understood, ma'am. I will stand by until otherwise ordered."

"Very good," said Balance with a nod. "I'll explain the mission particulars to Major Canopus now. Major Sirius, you're dismissed."

"Yes, Colonel." Lina had wanted to explain the situation directly to Canopus herself, but she had no confidence that doing so wouldn't renew her burning desire to go to Japan, so she did as she was told and left the room.

* * *

"—That is all. Do you have any questions, Major Canopus?" Balance asked, after explaining the circumstances of the missing missiles slated for disposal and the intelligence from the Seven Sages that Lina had provided.

"No, Colonel."

The only source for the existence of an imminent terrorist threat to Japan was a tip from the mysterious Seven Sages, whose status as an ally and reliable source was questionable at best. The question from the colonel carried the nuance of asking whether Canopus was really not dissatisfied with being sent on this mission based on such nebulous intel, but his answer relayed neither dissatisfaction nor question.

"I see. In that case, Major Canopus, *I* have a question for *you*."

"Yes, Colonel. What is it?"

Balance looked carefully at Canopus's expression, but there was no agitation to be found in it. Balance found this more a relief than a disappointment as she carefully phrased her question. "Major Canopus—or perhaps in this case I should say Major Benjamin Lowes."

Canopus's eyebrows flicked up slightly as Balance corrected herself.

"Are you related to Kane Lowes, the assistant to the president's deputy chief of staff?"

"Ma'am, as I believe you're aware, the assistant to the deputy chief of staff's father and my father are cousins, and his mother and mine are second cousins."

In other words, there was consanguineous marriage within the Lowes family, but marriages of such distance were not uncommon among aristocracy.

"The truth is, that wasn't all the information we received from the Seven Sages. I wish I could say it's a mistake, but…"

Canopus's expression shifted slightly at Balance's hesitation. *It can't be*, his face seemed to say.

"The assistant to the deputy chief of staff facilitated the release and export of the weapons that were due to be disposed of, as well as the departure of the terrorist himself from the country."

"…Could the assistant have been bribed?" he asked.

Balance shook her head sadly in response. "I'd feel a little better if that were the case, but…"

"So there are concerns beyond that?"

Balance grimaced, seeming almost reluctant to continue. "There's a high probability that the assistant to the deputy chief of staff was not bribed, but rather that he and a powerful member of Congress connected to him are attempting to use Gide Hague."

Canopus's shock was obvious.

Balance regarded him and posed a question seemingly unrelated to the matter at hand. "Major, what do you think of humanists?"

Humanism was a (heretical) offshoot of Christian religion that paraded the anti-magic ideology that "humans ought to live by only the power they were given." This, however, was only a fig leaf for their anti-magician activities.

But Canopus's answer was much more straightforward.

"I think it's mass hysteria. But I do think we need to be watchful for anyone who would try to manipulate the movement for their own ends."

"You don't feel threatened as a magician?"

"If it escalates any further, I do think we'll need to consider some way to deal with the movement. We magicians have no obligation to stand by while we're unjustly maligned."

"…You have rather extreme ideas, Major."

"Don't misunderstand me, Colonel. I merely believe that it's harmful to society for people not to exercise their right to self-defense. We mustn't take lightly the risk of the national division that could come from humanist discrimination on the part of these people calling themselves victims."

"I understand your political position. I've no intention of making it an issue here." Despite her lack of objection, her expression was very tense. "Mr. Lowes, the assistant to the deputy chief of staff, seems to share your conclusion, although via a different method. He believes that if the humanists are left alone any longer, they pose a serious threat to national security."

Balance studied the expression on Canopus's face carefully, but it remained almost infuriatingly cool and neutral.

"However, ours is a free country. We have to preserve freedom of speech to the greatest possible degree. No matter the principle being espoused, we must not suppress free speech. Or at least, that's what the politicians think."

"I quite agree, Colonel."

"…Which is why the group working with the assistant to the deputy chief of staff is plotting to direct the attention of the humanists abroad."

"They think having the humanists stage a terrorist attack in Japan will satisfy their hunger for violence?" Canopus's smirk was cold.

"Don't be snide, Major. It wasn't *my* idea," objected Balance, looking displeased.

"My apologies, Colonel," he said sincerely.

Balance continued without pressing the apology, feeling that perhaps she'd been a bit too sensitive herself. "If the information we got from the Seven Sages is good, Lowes's group's real goal isn't the terrorist attack itself."

"Meaning…?"

"It's impossible to perfectly limit the targets injured in a terrorist attack that uses explosives. Some of the victims will always be innocent bystanders."

"You don't mean…" Canopus's expression betrayed emotion for the first time.

"The blast from a portable missile launcher won't be enough to fatally injure a high-level magician unless they're caught totally off guard. But if they make a few dozen bombs out of the missiles' warheads and detonate them simultaneously, blocking the resulting explosion would be difficult even for Japan's Ten Master Clans. A high-level magician could avoid injury using a heat-resistant barrier, but civilian bystanders won't have that option. And with explosions coming from several directions at once, it won't be possible for third parties to protect everybody. The result will be casualties among not just magicians but also the general populace. That's the possible scenario the Seven Sages brought to our attention."

"And the attention of the humanists would be drawn to these Japanese magicians who let innocent bystanders die. Their energy would be directed toward Japan, and they'd spend less effort on anti-magician activities here. That would in turn decrease the risk of the humanists turning militant and destabilizing society—is that it?"

"Exactly."

Canopus's eyes glittered with a keen light. "So my mission is to intercept Gide Hague and prevent the terrorist attack?"

"I wish very much that that were the case," spat Balance, frustrated. "Ever since the parasite incident last year, the Japanese authorities have been watching us very carefully. It is quite likely that entering Japan and capturing Gide Hague without them knowing is impossible. If our actions are discovered, they would naturally pry into what our reason for capturing him is. And then they would discover in due time that a terrorist was using weapons that our military handed over."

"But if the attack is successful, won't they also still trace the weapons back to us? That's obviously a less desirable situation than preventing the attack, but—"

"There's a large difference between terrorists having obtained the missing weapons via a broker and the terrorists having stolen the weapons directly from us."

"…So you're suggesting we stand back and let the Japanese die?"

"I have already used a private back channel to warn them that a terrorist group headed by Gide Hague is attempting to infiltrate Japan."

Canopus couldn't entirely agree with Balance's position. But he couldn't deny that the USNA military needed to protect its own position. He was a soldier first and a magician second. That was the greatest difference between himself and the good-natured Lina, who was a magician first and a soldier second.

"Major, your mission is to assassinate Gide Hague, either before or after he executes his plan. Killing Hague may not stop the attack, but that's not your concern. According to the intel from the Seven Sages, Hague refuses to use air travel. If he's in international waters, you don't even have to be particularly discreet. You must not let him be captured by the Japanese."

"Understood."

Balance met Canopus's crisp salute with a guilty look. "I'm sorry, Major. I'm well aware that dirty work like this shouldn't be your job, but because there's a high probability that your target is an unusual magician, we need to send one of our best to meet him."

Canopus relaxed his salute and shook his head with a sad smile. "Your concern is unnecessary, Colonel. In fact, I should be thanking you. When I think about the high commander…about Lina…it makes me want to spare her from such gruesome work."

Canopus saluted again, then left the base commander's office.

Canopus arrived at the Yokosuka Joint U.S.-Japan Base on January 29 at 6:00 PM local time.

During the Twenty Years' Global War Outbreak, all American troops stationed in Japan had been recalled, and ever since then there were no American military bases remaining in the country. However, after the United States became the USNA, the Japanese-American alliance continued on in a different form. Bases that each nation could freely use were mutually established in both nations. Yokosuka Base was one of them. (All this being said, the Japanese armed forces practically never used the joint bases that existed within USNA borders.)

Naturally, the fact that Canopus, commander of the Stars' First Unit, had arrived in Japan was a secret. He proceeded directly to a USNA Navy destroyer that was about to leave port, which immediately headed offshore.

The destroyer carrying Canopus proceeded south toward Sagaminada and made a close pass by a small, twenty-meter yacht in the water between the Bousou Peninsula and the island of Ooshima. The moment the two vessels were closest to each other, Canopus *jumped* from the destroyer to the yacht, cloaked in optical camouflage magic that scattered both visible light and infrared. Stratospheric surveillance cameras might have caught this moment, but all they'd see was a vague blur—far from enough to make a positive identification. Thus did Canopus safely smuggle himself into Japan.

The yacht was a pleasure vessel used by upper-level bureaucrats at the USNA embassy, but its engine and outer hull were upgraded for espionage purposes as well. Naturally, it also had a state-of-the-art sensor package. It carried no weapons, but with Canopus aboard that was not remotely a concern.

Canopus directed the yacht around toward Sagaminada, heading south to wrap around the Izu Peninsula, then north into Suruga Bay. Owing to the leisurely cruising speed, it was the middle of the night before Canopus caught sight of the vessel he was looking for.

It was a small cargo ship, its deck completely covered by a roof of photovoltaic panels. To generate additional electricity while underway, arms on both sides of the hull would swing out, unfolding two additional solar panels that were highly reminiscent of the winglike pectoral fins of a flying fish. As an additional power source, the ship also carried a parallel internal photocatalytic hydrogen fuel cell so that it derived nearly all of its motive power from solar energy, and it was a fine example of the low-cost freighters that had come to dominate marine transport in the latter half of the twenty-first century.

Ever since Gide Hague has been suspected of having left the USNA, this ship had been identified as the likeliest choice for transport. But the ship had been expected to arrive in Japan yesterday, so the possibility of raiding the vessel while it was in international waters was abandoned, and Canopus's superiors instead decided to locate the port where it had anchored.

"Is that the ship, Major?" asked the USNA naval officer serving as captain of Canopus's yacht in a voice that was a mixture of awe and fear. As a temporary subordinate of Canopus during the mission, he'd been briefed on the major's background and circumstances. The Stars were already a legendary military unit, and Canopus was a member who'd been given a code name of the highest grade. The officer didn't seem aware that Canopus was the number two after Sirius, but what he did know was enough to make him obviously nervous. If he'd known Canopus's real rank, he probably wouldn't have been able to focus well enough to do his job.

Canopus gave a self-deprecating smile. It was such a disarming, open expression that he could practically feel the captain relax a little upon seeing it. "Unfortunately, ships are outside my expertise. I imagine you all are more used to identifying hull types than I am."

Beneath the remark was the implicit question: *Isn't a positive ID something your subordinates have already done?*

The captain straightened immediately. "Pardon me, sir. Yes, that is the vessel."

"I trust you, of course," said Canopus with a serious nod.

The captain breathed a sigh of relief.

"Captain—" Canopus dropped his smile and spoke in a tone befitting his expression.

"Yes, Major?"

"Keep that ship under observation. The fact that it went all the way from Yokosuka to Numazu means that he might be planning to use it again to escape."

"Understood, sir. I'll inform our field agents."

"We'll keep watch on it from here tonight."

"You're not going ashore, Major?"

"The window of opportunity for that has passed. We have to keep our risk of being exposed as low as we possibly can."

"Yes, sir!"

Canopus nodded wordlessly, then turned his gaze back to the freighter.

Balance had convinced Lina to take the high road and give up on going to Japan. Lina also felt that it wasn't a mistake to let Canopus handle the mission. He was a veteran combat magician, and Heavy Metal Burst notwithstanding, he was probably stronger than even Sirius. Lina reminded herself that there was almost no chance he'd botch the mission.

And yet, she couldn't stand sitting around and doing nothing.

"...I'm not getting involved. I'm staying here and behaving myself. So...it shouldn't be a problem if I contact an acquaintance to warn them. I deserve that much!"

Lina was alone, with nobody around to listen to her talking to herself, but she hastily revised *acquaintance* to *friend* nevertheless. She was clearly extremely self-conscious as she glanced back and forth, red-faced.

Realizing that she was acting a bit childishly, Lina cleared her throat—an affectation that itself was very endearing—and turned to face her visiphone's console.

The local time was 2:00 AM. This meant she'd stayed up until the wee hours agonizing over the problem but also that it was 6:00 PM in Japan. She hadn't planned it like this, but the timing was just right.

Having made the decision to call when the moment came to actually do it, her hesitation came back with renewed vigor. There, in front of the visiphone console, she resummoned her resolve and punched in Miyuki's number.

After five rings, the screen lit up. There on the display appeared the image of her rival's face, whose breathtaking beauty seemed to have only grown in the year since Lina had last seen her.

"Oh! Lina! Goodness, it's been a while." Miyuki merely looked at her without any sense of jealousy, fear, flattery, or admiration. Lina felt a strange sensation, as though a layer of ice covering her heart suddenly cracked.

"Hi, Miyuki. Long time no see! How've you been?"

"Reasonably well—thank you for asking. Have you lost weight, Lina? Are you okay? Is work keeping you too busy?"

Miyuki unceremoniously lumped both Lina's position as high commander of the Stars and her duties as Sirius together under the term *work*. Lina found the honest frankness refreshing.

"If anything, I've gotten heavier! Gosh, maybe I put on muscle?"

"Hmm…you must be in great shape. I'm envious."

"Miyuki…you know when you say things like that, I can't help but hear it as sarcasm. And anyway, what's the big idea getting even hotter? Just how much more gorgeous do you have to become before you're satisfied?"

"Now I think you're the one being sarcastic… But if I look any better, it must be Tatsuya's influence."

Lina was suddenly exhausted. She felt a pang of disappointment: *Honestly, if it weren't for this one thing…*

"Speaking of which, I heard you and Tatsuya are engaged. Congratulations."

"Thank you, Lina. News certainly does travel quickly."

"I mean, this is the princess of *the* Yotsuba family we're talking about here. People are going to be interested."

"Are they? So is that by any chance why you're calling—to congratulate me?"

For a moment, Lina was totally wrong-footed by Miyuki's delighted, happy smile, but then she remembered her real reason for calling. "Um, yeah, no, sorry. That's not it, actually."

In response to Lina's apology, Miyuki cocked her head, her expression turning quizzical rather than displeased. *"Goodness, it must be something important."*

Stop looking at me with such an adorable expression! Lina wanted to quip, but she resisted the urge. "Yeah, it's pretty important."

"...Should I go get my brother?"

Lina thought about it for less than a second, then nodded at Miyuki's suggestion. "Yeah, it'd probably be good for Tatsuya to hear this, too."

"All right, hang on."

The screen switched to the hold pattern. About thirty seconds later, Miyuki's lovely form reappeared. Sitting next to her was Tatsuya. To Lina's surprise, the distance between them was not zero.

"Hello, Lina. It's been a while," said Tatsuya.

"Hi, Tatsuya. It has."

"I'd love to chat, but Miyuki said you have something urgent to tell us. We can catch up another time, so let's hear the important part now."

"You haven't changed, Tatsuya. Always straight to the point—I like that," Lina blurted out, then inwardly winced. Saying things like *I like that* to Tatsuya's face was exactly the sort of phrasing that was like pouring jet fuel onto the flames when she considered Miyuki's penchant for bouts of jealousy.

But contrary to Lina's expectations, Miyuki remained calm.

It unnerved Lina.

"Um...Miyuki, you're not going to get mad?"

"Hmm? Mad at what?" Miyuki responded, her expression honestly befuddled. To her, it was obvious that Tatsuya would be appealing to other women, so there was no need to raise a fuss about such a small comment. But Lina didn't know that.

"Er, never mind." If she wasn't going to get snapped at, that was good enough for Lina. She counted herself lucky and moved on to the actual topic of her call. "Tatsuya, Miyuki—do you remember the Seven Sages?"

Tatsuya and Miyuki shared a look.

"*We remember,*" answered Tatsuya. "*Have you gotten some kind of information from them?*" he asked, picturing the face of Raymond S. Clark. He didn't think Lina knew the Sages' true identity nor that Raymond was one of them.

"I have, in fact." Not keen eyed enough to see through his poker face and lacking any telepathic magic, she interpreted his question at face value and answered it as such. "According to my information, a survivor from Dahan is planning a terrorist attack in Japan. The mastermind's name is Gide Hague. His Chinese name is Gu Jie. He's a survivor of the Kunlun Institute, and we can surmise that he's a magician, so... Miyuki, what's the matter?"

At the mention of Gu Jie's name, Miyuki had nearly cried out but then stifled herself. Lina didn't fail to take notice.

The truth was that she'd been shocked to hear the name of someone Raymond had told them last year was another of the Seven Sages, but as Tatsuya had shown no reaction at all, Miyuki quickly said, "*The Kunlun Institute is particularly significant to my family...but I apologize for interrupting.*"

"Oh, I see..."

Lina knew that the Yotsuba clan had some kind of a connection to the Kunlun Institute. She decided it wasn't surprising that the successor to the family's leadership would be dismayed to hear about a survivor from it and harbored no further doubts.

"You may have already guessed this, but I believe there's a high probability that Hague's target is the Yotsuba family."

"*I see. I agree, that's plausible. That's why you contacted Miyuki?*"

"Er—uh, yeah, I suppose it is." Lina found herself senselessly flustered at the revelation that Tatsuya agreed with her.

"*Neither Miyuki nor I can pretend this has nothing to do with us, it's true. It's even possible Miyuki's being directly targeted...*"

"Tatsuya...you really don't think about yourself much, do you? It's just as likely Hague's targeting you, you know," said Lina with an exasperated eye roll.

"If he comes after me, that would be considerably more convenient," Tatsuya noted, his expression fearless.

"…Yeah, good point. That would move things right along, wouldn't it?" Lina admitted, quite convinced.

Lina still didn't know what the nature of Tatsuya's true power was. She'd once suspected that he was an illusionist specializing in mental interference magic, but ever since they'd fought together against the parasites, she'd gotten the feeling that wasn't the answer.

In other words, to Lina, Tatsuya was an unknown quantity as a magician. But she had no doubt that he was considerably powerful. She found it difficult to imagine that he was in any danger of being beaten by a magician who had to rely on obsolete missiles to do harm to his enemies.

"Lina, what happened? You look like all your worries just suddenly disappeared," said Miyuki.

Lina's heart started racing at Miyuki's observation. Why did she have to be so relieved at the confirmation that Tatsuya wasn't in danger? "Uh, well, you know—"

The roar of her pounding heart made it hard to form words.

"I don't know, actually."

Lina felt a surge of irritation at Tatsuya's awkward smile. "C'mon! I mean, you know, with Hague and all, I just—"

—*wanted to tell you he was coming*, she was about to say but managed to clamp her mouth shut before she blurted it out.

"Oh… You were in a rush because you wanted to tell us about Hague, but now that you've done it, you're relieved."

"Yes, that!" Lina dramatically reached for the life preserver Tatsuya had thrown her. And then: "Oh, dear…"

Lina turned red right before Tatsuya and Miyuki's eyes.

"I see. Thanks, Lina," said Tatsuya, thanking her while ignoring her blush.

"Y-you don't need to thank me! I just wouldn't have been able to sleep at night if I stood by and did nothing, that's all! Anyway, talk to you later, Tatsuya, Miyuki! Good night!" Lina said at a rapid-fire pace before ending the call, completely forgetting about the time difference.

She took off the clothes she'd hastily thrown on and crawled back into bed without even putting on pajamas.

[5]

Six days had passed since Tatsuya and Miyuki received the call from Lina, making today Monday. There had been no further clues about Hague or the terrorist attack. And that was true for more than just them—neither Maya's people nor Canopus had made any progress in their search for Hague.

It was now February 4. The Master Clans Council would begin in two weeks.

The council was a summit for Japanese magical society. Even ancient magic practitioners who refused to recognize the Ten Master Clans as leaders of all magic society couldn't deny the event's influence. In particular, the Master Clans Selection Conference that would decide the composition of the Ten Master Clans was scheduled for the second day, which only heightened the attention Japan's magicians paid the overall event.

The students of First High, too, were abuzz. Despite still being mere students, they couldn't afford to ignore such important current events as people who were soon going to be making their way in the world as magicians themselves. In particular, any student connected to the Ten Master Clans or the Eighteen Support Clans found it impossible to concentrate on anything else, so consuming were their worries over whether their family would be selected for—or dropped from—the Ten.

This awareness was widespread among the First High student body, so when Miyuki arrived in the Class 2-A classroom as usual that morning, the other students seemed to somehow stiffen as they fell silent.

"Good morning, Shizuka, Honoka." As always, Miyuki greeted Shizuku, who sat in front of her, and Honoka, who stood next to Shizuku.

"Miyuki?! Why are you at school?!" Honoka's question was nearly a shout. That seemed to break the spell, and the whole classroom erupted in chatter.

"Why am I…? Today's a weekday, isn't it? Isn't it obvious why a high school student would be at school? Or have I been left out of the loop on something? Am I being bullied?" Miyuki placed a single hand to her cheek in an expression of the mildest concern.

At this, Honoka's eyes flashed in utter bewilderment. Shizuku was stunned silent, unsure of how to proceed.

But the pair's confusion did not last long.

"I'm sorry, I'm kidding." Miyuki giggled. "You thought I'd be absent, right? Because of the Master Clans Council starting today?"

"Y-yes!" Having rebooted, Honoka pressed Miyuki on the issue. "Can you afford not to be there, Miyuki? There's a Master Clans Selection Conference this year, right? As a future head of one of the families, shouldn't you—? Oh…"

Honoka slapped her hand over her mouth with an expression that said *oops*.

The rest of Miyuki's eavesdropping classmates all averted their gazes.

"You really don't need to worry about me so much…" Miyuki flashed a perplexed-looking smile. She couldn't help but be concerned about her classmates, who'd been walking on eggshells around her until that moment.

"So, Miyuki— Are you sure you don't need to go?" It was Shizuku who broke the tension, seemingly taking Miyuki at her word and asking the question without trying to overanalyze anything.

"I mean, I wasn't asked to," Miyuki said with a smile, which earned her a number of questioning looks. "I suppose you and Honoka might not have known this, Shizuku. The Master Clans Council's location is kept secret from everybody except the attendees. As of right now, even the people from the Eighteen Support Clans attending the Master Clans Selection Conference on the second day only know the general vicinity of where to go but not the precise meeting chamber they'll use."

"But, Miyuki, you're…"

Miyuki smiled brightly at Honoka, who was obviously taken aback. The words froze in Honoka's throat. "I haven't been asked to attend, so I don't know where the conference is. It's not that I don't care about what's being discussed, but without even a vague sense of where it's happening, I can't very well go, can I?"

"Yeah, that's true." It was Shizuku who replied, nodding at the point. Honoka was still red-faced and speechless.

Meanwhile, a similar uproar was happening in Class 2-E.

"Huh? Tatsuya, what're you doing at school?"

"That's a weird way to say good morning, Mizuki. Also, good morning."

"Uh…um… Sorry about that."

Tatsuya wasn't particularly annoyed, but it was a natural thing for him to say. He was a high school student and hadn't been absent because of a long bout of illness, so it struck him as nonsensical to be asked why he was at school on an ordinary Monday.

But Mizuki wasn't the only person that day to have abandoned common sense.

As soon as the classroom window facing the hallway rattled open, Erika poked her head in. "Hey, Tatsuya, should you be at school?!" she shouted without any preamble whatsoever.

"Erika…why is everybody trying to make me go away?" Tatsuya frowned while next to him, Mizuki looked down, embarrassed, which did not go unnoticed by Erika.

"Ha! Ha-ha-ha-ha-ha-ha!" Realizing her own actions had been a *bit* odd, Erika burst out in nervous laughter in an obvious attempt to muddy the waters, even knowing she was being ridiculous.

But fortunately for Erika, she wasn't the only one who was stepping into the minefield. "But seriously, Tatsuya, today's the Master Clans Council, right? Should you be going?" Leo wondered.

"Why would you need to ask me something like that?" Tatsuya asked. He wasn't being obtuse; he seemed genuinely perplexed.

"I think it would more strange if we didn't care at all," Erika answered, at which Leo nodded his agreement.

It privately occurred to Tatsuya that those two were getting along rather well. "But why?" he shot back. "I mean, I know a lot of people are thinking about it, but…" He glanced back over his shoulder, and his classmates all hastily looked elsewhere. "If you think that me being connected to the Yotsuba family is reason enough, you're mistaken. Just being related to one of the Ten Master Clans doesn't mean you can participate in the conference. As the acting head of the Juumonji family, Katsuto Juumonji is obviously attending, but I don't believe Mayumi Saegusa has ever gone."

"…Oh yeah?" Leo looked deflated. Erika, on the other hand, seemed satisfied with the explanation.

"And even if I knew where the conference was, I wouldn't have any desire to go. I'd just be sitting around with nothing to do, so coming to school and studying is a far better use of my time."

"But, like, don't you care about what they're talking about at the conference?"

"Nonparticipants aren't allowed in the meetings, so even if I was there, it wouldn't matter. And not even all the meeting results are made public. There's no way of knowing how the arguments developed."

Leo sighed. "So in the end, we have to just go along with whatever they announce, huh?"

"That's how it is."

If the conversation had ended there, it could have been filed away under ordinary small talk.

But then—

The room had fallen quiet as Tatsuya's classmates listened carefully, but one voice—rather loudly for someone who seemed to be talking to himself—rang out. "So basically, us powerless nobody magicians just have to do what you decide? What a very Master Clans thing to say."

Its source was diagonally behind Tatsuya. More precisely, it came from diagonally behind Mizuki.

"What, you got something you wanna say?" Erika glared sharply at Chiaki Hirakawa, the student who'd spoken up.

Chiaki didn't answer Erika's question. Not only that, she appeared to be deliberately looking away.

Erika's eyes narrowed. Poking her head in the window, Erika then moved to enter through the door and approach the girl.

"Wait, hold on, Chiba. Just calm down!" One of the students hurriedly moved to block her path.

It was Tomitsuka who stood up in an attempt to protect (?) peace in the classroom. He wasn't actually the class representative but seemed to have assumed those duties somehow anyway.

"Tomitsuka, would you step aside? I have some words for that girl."

"No, you really shouldn't!" Tomitsuka understood perfectly well what Erika meant by *words* as he desperately tried to talk her down.

But then Chiaki stood, as though determined to waste his efforts. "What? You know it's true."

"What's true? Huh?"

The two girls stared daggers at each other over Tomitsuka's shoulder.

"Chiba, look, class is gonna start soon…" Tomitsuka tried to mediate, having made himself a shield as he stood in front of Chiaki.

But he was immediately crushed. "There's still five minutes. So, Hirakawa—what was it you were saying was true, hmm?"

The ferocity in Erika's eyes was enough to make even most of the boys in the class shiver.

"That he's related to one of the Ten Master Clans! I didn't say a thing that isn't true!" Chiaki shot back resolutely, despite her own knees also quivering.

"Huh? Yeah, so it turns out Tatsuya's related to one of the Ten. But so what? Just because someone's parents are in the Ten doesn't mean their children are."

"You think that kind of technicality matters? The reality is, he's part of the Yotsuba family, and he hid it and lied to all of us!"

"I guess a spoiled little rich girl like you from a normal family wouldn't understand, but among magicians there are a lot of kids who don't get to take their parents' names, you know."

Chiaki didn't have an immediate retort ready. What Erika was saying was true, and Chiaki realized that she'd only known about it in the abstract. "W-well, why…"

"Hmm? If you've got something to say, go ahead and spit it out!"

Erika's scorn inflamed Chiaki's rage. Her fury burned out the brakes of her good sense. "Why are you even getting mad about this for him?! Are you in love with him or something?!"

The two girls' onlooking classmates all winced. Chiaki's implication would have been an insult to the dignity of any contemporary high school student. The rude comeback would have been something like, *Who likes who doesn't have anything to do with it—what're you, stupid?*

And so *What're you, stupid?* was exactly what Erika said: "Me, in love with *him*? I value my life a little more than that, sorry."

Her response, however, made the students of 2-E tilt their heads in confusion.

"I'm not gonna tempt fate by announcing myself as Miyuki's romantic rival, thanks. A literally life-threatening crush is gonna be a hard pass from me."

If Miyuki had overheard such a statement, it would not have gone over well. Even sympathizing with it would have been dangerous. But hearing this, all the onlookers in 2-E—everyone aside from Tatsuya, Chiaki, and Tomitsuka—nodded emphatically at Erika's words.

"God, I can't believe I got into a fight with someone *this* dumb," Erika declared, turning around and striding toward the classroom's exit. "I'm going back to my class, Tatsuya. See you."

"Yeah, later," Tatsuya said with a wave and a pleasant smile as Erika left 2-E's classroom.

In the end, Chiaki had successfully repelled Erika's attack. But as Chiaki stood there, she trembled in humiliation.

For high school students, the Master Clans Council was essentially a source of recreational argument, but for the adults participating in it, the event was a deadly serious struggle; it was nothing less than a negotiation with lives on the line.

The venue was a conference room in a relatively luxurious hotel in Hakone. As the meeting's commencement time approached, the seats at the roundtable began to fill up.

There was Gouki Ichijou, the head of the Ichijou family, wearing a rough sweater over his dark, copper, well-tanned skin, every inch of his tall frame that of a man of the sea. He had come from his residence in Kanazawa, having recently celebrated his forty-second birthday. His public persona was that of the president of an undersea resource exploration conglomerate.

The attractive middle-aged woman in an expensive kimono with her hair in an elegant arrangement was Mai Futatsugi, the head of the Futatsugi family. She was fifty-five years old and resided in Ashiya.

Her public face was that of a majority shareholder in a variety of industrial chemical and food-related companies.

Wearing a polo shirt and sport coat and based out of Atsugi was Gen Mitsuya. Compactly and sturdily built, he was fifty-three years old. Whether it was public or not was a matter of some question, but in any case, he was an international small arms broker.

The beautiful woman in the formal wine-colored gown was the head of the Yotsuba family, Maya. She looked like she couldn't be a day older than thirty, although in reality she was forty-seven.

In a simple and tidy business suit was the head of the Itsuwa family, Isami Itsuwa, forty-nine, from Uwajima. He was known to the public as an executive and owner of a maritime shipping company.

With her chestnut-brown hair trimmed in a short bob, the glamorous woman wearing a pantsuit was Atsuko Mutsuzuka, head of the family of the same name. Atsuko was twenty-nine and resided in Sendai. Publicly, she owned a geothermal energy exploration firm.

The head of the Saegusa family, Kouichi, was dressed stylishly retro, like an elite businessman from the 1980s or 1990s. He was forty-eight and lived in Tokyo. Notably, his light brown–tinted glasses did not come off even inside. Publicly, he was a venture capitalist.

Wearing a suit *sans* necktie and sporting short hair with a slightly upswept side part was the head of the Yatsushiro family, Raizou, thirty-one, from Fukuoka. His public face was that of a university instructor and a majority shareholder in several telecommunication firms.

The white-haired gentleman in the foreign-branded three-piece suit was Makoto Kudou, head of the Kudou family. He was sixty-four, from Ikoma. The public knew him as a financier and shareholder in various munitions companies.

The man with the shaved head in traditional *haori* jacket and *hakama* was Kazuki Juumonji, head of the Juumonji family, forty-four, from Tokyo. Publicly, he owned an excavation and construction firm that primarily served the armed forces.

These were all the heads of the current Ten Master Clans. Only Kazuki Juumonji had brought a second: his son Katsuto.

The heads all sat at the roundtable, and the door closed. The youngest person present, Katsuto, locked the door.

It was the oldest, Makoto Kudou, who spoke first. "Mr. Juumonji, are you feeling better?"

The Ten Master Clans were peers and equals—there was no hierarchy. This fact was clear from the use of the roundtable in the hotel meeting room.

But problems could arise in conducting a meeting without a chairperson, so it was an unwritten tradition that the oldest member present acted as the meeting's facilitator.

Makoto had begun by inquiring after Kazuki Juumonji's health because Kazuki had been absent from several recent meetings, having sent his son Katsuto in his stead. This was the first time in three years that the other heads had seen Kazuki in person.

"Regarding that, I have an announcement to make." At Makoto's prompt, Kazuki stood. Deliberation among the Ten Master Clans typically took place while sitting, so this gesture indicated that what came next would be important.

"This may seem sudden, but I, Kazuki Juumonji, do hereby transfer the leadership of the Juumonji family to my son Katsuto. As such, I ask that you all bear witness to this act."

The other heads all reacted variously—some looking to their neighbors, others watching Kazuki closely. What they all had in common, however, was that not a one spoke up.

"Well, that certainly is a rather sudden announcement," Makoto said eventually, finally putting the general mood of the table into words.

"I have considered the matter for some time. I had hoped to wait until Katsuto reached the age of majority, but I feel it does neither the Juumonji family nor the Ten Master Clans any credit for me, a man who's no longer any use as a magician, to continue as head."

"When you say you can't use magic, what do you mean?" It was Gouki Ichijou who asked. He was often the one who voiced difficult questions in these meetings.

"For the past three years, I have suffered a condition that has diminished my ability to use magic. By two years ago, I was no longer able to withstand the rigors of combat, and I entrusted Katsuto with the practical duties of acting as family head. Then three months ago, my magical faculties disappeared entirely."

A murmur ran through the room at this bombshell.

"A condition that reduces magical ability? This is the first I've heard of such a thing. You'll pardon my rudeness, but this is a matter of grave concern to all magicians. Are the details of the illness known? Is there a treatment?" pressed Kouichi Saegusa. He was always among the most verbose of the Master Clans Council participants.

"There is no need to worry on that count, Mr. Saegusa. This disease is confined to the Juumonji family."

"It's specific to your family? Are you certain of that?"

"Mr. Saegusa." Maya cut Kouichi off with a smooth, unruffled tone of voice. "I would gently suggest that you needn't press any further."

"Yes, we don't pry too deeply into the matters of other families. That goes not just for the Juumonji family but for magicians in general. As Ms. Yotsuba suggests, perhaps you should let this go. Mr. Juumonji has already said that this is not something other families need worry about, so should we not leave it at that?" Mai Futatsugi added. As the council's second-eldest member, she often took it upon herself to end long debates.

"Understood. Please accept my apologies, Mr. Juumonji." Kouichi had no reason to be so stubborn as to go up against both Maya *and* Mai.

"Not at all," Kazuki noted to him before turning to the women and nodding his thanks. "Now then, are we all satisfied with the issue of the Juumonji succession?"

"I believe that the Juumonji family may decide such things for itself, regardless of this council's presence," Maya stated. "That said, I have no qualms. I'm entirely happy to act as a witness for Katsuto's succession."

"I don't mind at all, either," said Atsuko Mutsuzuka, picking up where she left off. "Quite the contrary—I would be honored to serve as a witness."

Atsuko was known to look up to Maya, and when there were disagreements, she often sided with her. The fact that the eldest son of the Shibata family, one of the Yotsuba branch families, had formerly attended Fifth High School in Sendai was also not irrelevant.

"I have no intention of quibbling over another family's choice of successor. I welcome Katsuto's assumption of the position. Kazuki's condition is unfortunate, but the magic community still owes him a debt for his long service," Kouichi said, emphatically voicing his support, feeling a need to make his position extra-clear given what he'd said earlier.

With Maya and Kazuki both having accepted Kouichi's request, the remaining family heads each took their turn congratulating Katsuto and thanking Kazuki for his long service.

"Now then, Katsuto," Makoto said to wrap things up. "As the new head of the Juumonji family, please take your seat."

And thus, it was confirmed.

Kazuki left the room once his son dismissed him, and then the heads of the Ten Master Clans all took their seats.

The Master Clans Council was convened.

"Now then, Mr. Ichijou," Makoto prompted.

"There are no problematic developments in the Hokuriku and Sanin regions." Gouki nodded and began to outline the status of ongoing observation of anti-government activities and possible threats of infiltration. "We also haven't identified any evidence of planned incursions from either the New Soviet Union or the Great Asian Alliance."

"Ms. Mutsuzuka?"

"We've seen no unusual activity in the Tohoku region."

"Ms. Futatsugi."

"The Hanshin region is business as usual—a perfect eyesore I wish I could finally wipe clean."

"...Mind yourself, Ms. Futatsugi. Mr. Itsuwa."

"There is no conspicuous activity in the Shikoku region."

"Mr. Yatsushiro."

"The Kitakyushu region is business as usual, though perhaps not to the extent of the Hanshin area."

"I see. Do be vigilant."

These reports regarded the activity in the regions each family was responsible for. Magicians affiliated with the military considered the island of Hokkaido, the Ogasawara region, and the Okinawa Islands their turf, so the Ten Master Clans couldn't easily interfere there. Apart from those, the breakdown of responsibility was thus: The Hokuriku and Sanin regions were the Ichijou family's; the Tohoku region was the Mutsuzuka family's; the Hanshin and Chugoku regions were the Futatsugi family's; the Shikoku region was the Itsuwa family's; the Kyushu region (except for Okinawa) was the Yatsushiro family's; and the Kyoto, Nara, Shiga, and Kii regions were the Kudou family's. Meanwhile, along with other families associated with the number three, the Mitsuya family managed Lab Three, which continued to provide their expertise to the military's magicians.

The Saegusa and Juumonji families were responsible for the Kanto region, including Izu, and the Yotsuba kept watch over the Tokai, Gifu, and Nagano regions, as no other family was shouldering that responsibility.

"Mr. Saegusa."

"There has been an increase in anti-magician activity in the Kanto region. It hasn't yet reached a level where intervention is necessary, but I do believe we will need to get involved sooner rather than later. There has also been suspicious movement in the Yokosuka area. Saboteurs may be planning to breach the border."

"Do you concur with this, Mr. Juumonji?"

"As far as anti-magician activity goes, the Juumonji family shares Mr. Saegusa's assessment. Regarding sabotage, unfortunately we have not apprehended anyone."

"Hmm. We'll discuss these so-called humanists in more detail later. Next, Ms. Yotsuba?"

"We've seen nothing at the level of the Kanto region, but the humanists are making inroads into the Tokai area. Also, Mr. Saegusa, Mr. Juumonji—"

"What is it, Ms. Yotsuba?" replied Kouichi with a smile that had something besides good humor and politeness mixed into it. Interactions with Maya were the only time when Kouichi betrayed any sort of strong emotion.

For Maya's part, she showed no concern at his gaze. She always looked back at him with a completely unconcerned expression.

"There has been some suspicious activity around Izu. I propose that we strengthen surveillance there."

Maya stayed true to form. She merely glanced dismissively at Kouichi briefly before looking away at nothing in particular and giving a businesslike answer.

"Understood. Would you mind terribly, explaining more specifically what that activity entails?" Katsuto stated gravely. Despite being surrounded by people considerably his senior, he betrayed no diffidence whatsoever.

"Not at all, I would be happy to. Last week, a small freighter from North America docked at the Port of Yokosuka, and it is currently anchored at Numazu. A yacht operated by the USNA embassy is currently observing it. The yacht is presently cloaked, and its surveillance of the freighter appears ongoing."

"Ms. Yotsuba, do you know the precise whereabouts of this yacht?" Kouichi asked.

"I do not. I expect it's in international waters."

The reply might have seemed flippant, but this was a case Kouichi ought to have been investigating himself. The Juumonji family was more suited to providing emergency combat personnel. While they shared responsibility for the Kanto and Izu regions, it was the Saegusa family who was supposed to shoulder the burden of conducting investigations within the region.

Naturally, Kouichi understood this, and he smoothly summarized his plan for the situation. "In that case, our family will look into it, given the increase in anti-magician activity. If the freighter is carrying assets meant for humanist terrorist acts, the USNA authorities may be after it. Numazu is in the Yotsuba family's region of responsibility, but given that the freighter first arrived at Yokosuka, the Saegusa family will provide backup here."

"Indeed. Thank you for your cooperation." Maya nodded, leaving room for no further discussion of Hague's freighter or the yacht carrying Canopus.

With the traditional reports now delivered, the mood in the room shifted.

"Mr. Kudou, I have a matter I would like to bring to this council." It was, of course, Kouichi who spoke, and his words held the unmistakable whiff of trouble.

"Go ahead, Mr. Saegusa," Makoto said, seemingly stifling a sigh.

"In that case, I'll proceed. Thank you for your time," Kouichi prefaced, then looked to Maya.

A distinct sense of *not this again* seemed to emanate from both Atsuko Mutsuzuka and Raizou Yatsushiro. Kouichi's (always polite and gentlemanly) attacks on Maya were, it was fair to say, a perennial feature of the council.

"Ms. Yotsuba, my congratulations on selecting your successor."

"Thank you very much."

Both Kouichi and Maya wore superficially polite smiles. Behind Kouichi's was the provocatively piercing quality of his eyes, which was met by Maya's unflinchingly cold gaze. For some reason, both of them seemed to be on a war footing already.

"However, I find I cannot approve of the engagement between your son and your successor."

"What is that? It was my understanding that you consider personal matters such as marriage to be outside the purview of the Master Clans Council. Was I wrong?"

Kouichi replied before any assenting voices could interpose themselves. "Yes, for an ordinary marriage, I would not speak up as I have. However, it's a different matter when there is a risk of rare and precious magical talent being lost."

The eyes of everyone around the table, apart from Maya and Kouichi, were on Gouki Ichijou.

Gouki was frowning, his arms folded. From his expression, his inner monologue—*Why here of all places?*—was practically audible.

"What sort of effect will a consanguineous marriage have on the magic abilities of the children resulting from that marriage? Research into this problem has been ongoing for some time, but there are no firm conclusions yet. Some researchers say it would be harmless, and still others say it might have a beneficial effect. But so long as there's an appreciable risk of genetic abnormalities, marriage between closely related people has been considered undesirable. And in fact, among the Numbers, even marriage between cousins—which is legal—has been falling increasingly out of favor."

Makoto Kudou interlaced his fingers and closed his eyes. From the outside, it looked as though he was deep in thought.

"Whatever the trend is, the fact is that it's not prohibited. There is even precedent." The irritated voice that spoke up to dispute Kouichi did not belong to Maya.

"Yes, that's quite true, Mr. Yatsushiro. Just as you say, there are married cousins among the Twenty-Eight. However, in that case, the fathers were only half brothers from different mothers. You cannot equate that to the proposition Ms. Yotsuba has put before us."

Next it was Atsuko Mutsuzuka who objected to Kouichi's assertion. "It's relatively common to see cases of marriage between second cousins or instances where the groom is the bride's father's cousin. Despite the greater genetic distance, when these add up, is the risk not much the same as with a closer marriage?"

Despite Atsuko's eloquent point, Kouichi did not falter: "It's impossible to bring the risk to zero. This is entirely a question of degree, Ms. Mutsuzuka. My objection to the engagement of the Yotsuba family's successor is predicated on the fact that their mothers were identical twins, making this a match of cousins who are unusually close, genetically speaking. In other words, they are functionally half-siblings by different fathers."

Atsuko fell silent. If one ignored the emotional baggage he was clearly bringing to the discussion, his logic was persuasive.

"Marriage between cousins is permitted by law. However, if this is functionally a marriage between half-siblings, one could argue that this is an attempt to use a loophole to circumvent the law."

"Mr. Saegusa, that is going too far." It was Mai Futatsugi, speaking softly, who rebuked him for the implicit accusation embedded in his statement.

"My apologies. I indeed overstepped. Ms. Yotsuba, I ask your forgiveness."

Maya ignored Kouichi's apology. "So what is it you want to say, Mr. Saegusa?" she said instead, getting right to the point.

Kouichi paused his smoothly delivered position, and from his seat between Isami Itsuwa and Atsuko Mutsuzuka, he fixed his eyes on Maya's profile across the table. "What I want to say is very simple. I believe the engagement between Miyuki Shiba and Tatsuya Shiba should be annulled and withdrawn."

Maya turned to him.

The two stared each other down.

Behind the slightly tinted lenses he always wore, something flickered in Kouichi's one remaining eye—either exultation or loathing.

"I'm sorry, but may I interject here?" It was Gouki Ichijou who raised his voice and doused the rising tension between the other two.

"Our family has yet to receive an answer to our proposal from yours. I admit that it is not unrelated to what Mr. Saegusa has brought up."

"Are you referring to your proposal of an engagement between your Masaki and our Miyuki?"

"I am."

Maya, at first looking to Gouki, now turned away and let out an exhausted sigh. "Is Masaki not expected to become the head of the Ichijou family? Meanwhile, Miyuki will be assuming leadership of our family. Setting aside the impropriety of proposing an engagement to someone who's already engaged, I don't see how what you're suggesting is even worth considering," she said with a distinctly offended frigidity.

"I apologize for any offense. But our proposal is entirely sincere. We have no intention of mischief or harassment of any kind."

"Sincere? What part of *give us an already-engaged girl* could possibly seem sincere, I wonder?"

"My son sincerely hopes to be wed to Miyuki. If you were to accept our offer, it was my intention to send Masaki to join the Yotsuba family."

A murmur rippled around the table. Masaki Ichijou, also known as the Crimson Prince, was an exemplar of the Ten Master Clans. He'd demonstrated his prowess in combat when he was only thirteen, and during the Yokohama Incident of 2095, he'd proven himself worthy of his sobriquet. Now at barely seventeen, he was considered a top-tier combat magician.

Gouki was saying he was willing to let such an heir go. The Yotsuba family clearly stood to gain more from such an arrangement. Even Maya had to admit that there was no room in the proposal for an implied insult.

"I see. And yet, I am still unable to grant your request."

"...May I ask why not?"

"Mr. Ichijou, I can see that as a parent, you are trying to ensure your son's happiness. But just as you, his father, are keeping your son's feelings in mind, so too must I, Miyuki's aunt, respect *her* feelings on the matter."

"Miyuki's feelings on the matter?"

"Yes. My niece is very fond of my son Tatsuya, and it would be difficult to claim that he is indifferent toward her. I want to respect their wishes."

Mai Futatsugi and Atsuko Mutsuzuka both nodded firmly. Evidently, this particular matter was easier for women to sympathize with.

"And are Miyuki's feelings unlikely to change? Will she not even give Masaki a chance?"

"A chance?"

"It's my understanding that Miyuki hardly knows about Masaki at all."

"Is that not just as true of Masaki? Your son knows almost nothing about Miyuki save what she looks like."

Gouki winced at the implication—that his son was merely taken with Miyuki's beauty. But as he couldn't refute the point, he only pushed harder. "That is why I'd like to give them a chance to get to know each other. If after that, Miyuki doesn't choose Masaki, then our family will obediently withdraw."

"Mr. Ichijou…are you aware that you are being quite disrespectful to Miyuki, Tatsuya, and our family? And in particular to my son. I can't see any way to interpret your suggestion as anything other than implying that Tatsuya is less of a man than Masaki."

Gouki was at a loss for words. He hadn't meant to imply such a thing, but he suddenly realized that his affection for his own son had blinded him to the less-than-ideal implications.

Mai, who was normally the council member most likely to defuse tense situations, had no reproof for Maya's harsh words. This suggested that the majority of the assembled family heads agreed that Gouki was in the wrong.

And then Kouichi trotted out his own grievance again. "But if we set aside romantic feelings for a moment and consider this objectively, I believe that Masaki and Miyuki would make a far more favorable match. Above all, it avoids the potential risks of a consanguineous marriage."

Gen Mitsuya had listened without speaking thus far, but he finally raised his voice to chide Kouichi, his tone very displeased. "Mr. Saegusa, are you saying that Miyuki's feelings in this matter are irrelevant?"

But Kouichi persisted. "Sometimes it is necessary to set aside one's own feelings—particularly when one is the head of one of the Ten Master Clans. Has everyone here not had to do so at some point or another?"

No one raised an argument on this point. All present knew that Kouichi himself had done exactly this.

"And Miyuki is still very young. If she actually spends some time with Masaki, her heart may very well change."

"That is true... There are aspects of compatibility between men and women that can only be known through actual contact."

This was the first voice in support of Kouichi. It belonged to Isami Itsuwa. But it was Kouichi himself who was surprised at Isami's words. He was careful not to let it show on his face, but he was inwardly suspicious.

"I thought there was a good match to be made between Mr. Saegusa's eldest daughter and my eldest son, but Mayumi and Hirofumi's personalities did not mesh well, and in the end, it did not work out."

Just as Isami said, the marriage negotiations with the Itsuwa family had broken down just before the Master Clans Council.

"Mr. Saegusa's assertion that Masaki of the Ichijou and Miyuki of the Yotsuba would make for a favorable match is a logical one. Their marriage could bring about major advancements for Japanese magic. Given that the Ichijou family is willing to send Masaki to be adopted into the Yotsuba family, it doesn't strike me as a bad proposition for the Yotsuba family at all."

With Isami's support, the sea began to change. For that moment, Kouichi and Gouki finally had the wind at their backs.

But it only took an instant for that wind to die down.

"Mr. Itsuwa, my family is not seeking to gain anything through Miyuki's marriage."

Isami looked down shamefacedly. In one clipped refutation, Maya had clearly shown how his characterization was meant to direct the discussion toward the consideration of immediate gains and losses.

Maya continued. "Yes, it's true that Miyuki is still young. It is not impossible that her heart may change. But if that is your contention, Masaki ought to change her mind through his own efforts. If he has what it takes to steal Miyuki away from Tatsuya, I won't hold her back. The Yotsuba family will not see her married off, but I would be willing to give up the position of son-in-law to whomever she chooses."

"So you will not dissolve the engagement?"

"But in exchange, you won't object to Masaki pursuing Miyuki on his own?"

Makoto and Mai, respectively, spoke up to confirm Maya's position.

"I am content with that," said Maya. "And just to be clear, I'll point out for the record that Miyuki and Tatsuya's engagement is a legally valid one. There is nothing about it that demands we entertain any objections."

Mai nodded. "As you say, Ms. Yotsuba. It is a fact that consanguineous marriage involves risk. That said, Mr. Saegusa's objection exceeds the boundaries of the Master Clans Council's authority." Mai shifted her gaze across the table from Kouichi to Gouki, who sat next to her. "Is this acceptable to you, Mr. Ichijou? Ms. Yotsuba has stated that she'll allow your son to see Miyuki, despite her extant engagement. As his father, there is little more you can do for him."

"...Understood. I will tell my son as much."

Gouki and Kouichi abandoned their attack. Of course, Kouichi

was not the type to wave a white flag without extracting any concessions at all.

"Incidentally, does your willingness to allow contact and interaction despite the engagement extend to Tatsuya as well?" he asked with a smile, as Maya and Mai's gazes bored into him. "As Mr. Itsuwa said earlier, things with his son Hirofumi and my daughter Mayumi did not go well, you see. If it were to work out, I would not at all mind seeing Mayumi married to Tatsuya."

Though the late Retsu Kudou's magic technique had earned him the moniker "the Trickster," it seemed that Kouichi had quite a mischievous side himself.

The response around the table to Kouichi's malicious ploy was one of universal exhaustion, so the Master Clans Council temporarily adjourned. When it reconvened ten minutes later, Maya immediately dropped a bombshell. This was no mealymouthed argument about abstract principles, either, but a truly explosive revelation.

"I have something I'd like to bring to this council's attention," said Maya.

"Oh-ho. It's quite rare for you to bring a problem to us, Ms. Yotsuba. Whatever could it be, I wonder?" Makoto prompted.

Maya smiled pleasantly to Kouichi.

A shudder ran down the spines of everyone around the table except those two—even Katsuto, who had seen relatively little of the antagonism between them.

Maya's glistening, ruby-red lips slowly parted as she began. "Are you all aware of a man named Gongjin Zhou?"

The moment the words were out of her mouth, Makoto stiffened. Kouichi showed no reaction whatsoever, but that lack of reaction itself was something of a clue.

"Gongjin Zhou…?"

"I assume you're not talking about Gongjin Zhou as in the Wu general from the Three Kingdoms era."

Maya, still smiling, shook her head at Atsuko Mutsuzuka and Raizou Yatsushiro's respective questions. "No, he was a practitioner of ancient magic from the continent, who made Yokohama Chinatown his home base. Taoists, I believe they're called. Isn't that right, Mr. Kudou?"

"Er, yes. The ancient magicians from the continent are often referred to as such." Makoto was doing his utmost to keep his body from trembling.

"Mr. Kudou, are you quite all right? You look rather unwell."

"No, it's nothing, Ms. Mutsuzuka."

As Atsuko tilted her head curiously at Makoto, he turned his back to Maya. "So why do you bring up this Gongjin Zhou?"

"Blanche, the international anti-magic political group. The international crime syndicate No-Head Dragon. The military saboteurs from the Great Asian Alliance who were responsible for the Yokohama Incident. And the vampiric parasites in Tokyo that caused a worldwide uproar. Each of these brought chaos to our nation. That man was the mastermind who orchestrated all of those incidents—or, more accurately, the one to whom the real mastermind delegated Japanese operations."

A wave of unrest rippled through the meeting room.

There was no audible murmur that came with it—there were only ten people present, after all, and this was no trivial matter that anyone present would whisper to their neighbor about.

But the shock of Maya's statement was such that it stripped the heads of the Ten Master Clans of their composure.

"Ms. Yotsuba." Across from Maya, Raizou raised his hand lightly. His university classroom habits seemed to be coming out. "You said *delegated*, in the past tense. Is that because Gongjin Zhou has already been, ah, dealt with? Or is it because he has already fled Japan?"

"In October of last year, with the help of Masaki Ichijou and Minoru Kudou, Tatsuya brought him down."

Makoto was clearly surprised. While Masaki had told Gouki about the incident, Makoto had not heard about it from Minoru.

None of the other family heads noticed his surprise, however. Their attention was focused entirely on Maya, and apart from Kouichi, Gouki, and Makoto, they nodded, their expressions concerned.

"Minoru—that's your youngest son, correct?" said Raizou, who sat next to Makoto.

Makoto managed a polite smile and nod.

Gen Mitsuya offered effusive praise. "Masaki of the Ichijou family, Tatsuya of the Yotsuba family, and Minoru of the Kudou family... such a dauntless feat."

Mai Futatsugi concurred. "Indeed, it is. I'm overjoyed to see the next generation being raised to achieve such excellence. It bodes well for the future of Japan's magical community."

"For myself and Mr. Juumonji, they're not so much the next generation as they are our junior colleagues—but yes, their promise is clear." Atsuko Mutsuzuka's point elicited a smile from the older members.

However, the pleasant mood was quickly dispelled by Maya's next words.

"Mr. Saegusa—you conspired with Gongjin Zhou, did you not?"

A hush fell over the roundtable.

"...Do you have any factual basis whatsoever for that question, Ms. Yotsuba?" replied Isami Itsuwa in a hoarse, strangled voice.

Kouichi had yet to speak.

"Mr. Saegusa, there is ample evidence that through a subordinate, Saburou Nakura, you made contact with Gongjin Zhou, and in April of last year, you indirectly influenced Kanda, a Diet member from the Civil Rights party, to foment anti-magician activity. Do you deny this?"

Kouichi's reply was slow in coming. "I would also like to see your basis for these accusations, Ms. Yotsuba."

"If it's all right, I have a comment." It was the voice of Katsuto, the youngest person present, that rose in the tense atmosphere of the room. Undaunted by the eyes that swiveled to look at him, his voice was calm and even as he began his comment. "It is true that Mr.

Saegusa encouraged anti-magician activity. I heard as much from Mr. Saegusa himself."

The gazes falling on Katsuto turned toward Kouichi.

"Mr. Saegusa, is there an explanation for this?" asked Atsuko, her eyes sharp.

Kouichi smirked an unconcerned smile. "What Mr. Juumonji said is true. And what you've been told by Ms. Yotsuba is also largely true. But there seems to have been a misunderstanding about the order of events."

"The order of events? Explain yourself!" Gouki spat angrily.

Kouichi's smile remained. "It was only after the lull in anti-magician activity that followed the stellar reactor experiment at First High that I used a subordinate to contact Gongjin Zhou. Now that I think of it, that was another of Tatsuya's achievements for the Yotsuba family. The Rosen branch president was deeply impressed with the experiment, and the winds of change started to blow. He really is an admirable young man, your son."

"And what does that have to do with anything?" Gouki pressed, irritated.

Kouichi did not attempt to draw out his story any longer or otherwise provoke Gouki. "The reason I contacted Gongjin Zhou was to stop the mass media's attempts to treat magicians as a unified whole. Of course, I needed something to bargain with, but I didn't offer him anything that would have compromised the Japanese magical community."

"Ah yes, that's right. You cooperated with Gongjin Zhou after he incited anti-magician activity." Maya briskly agreed with Kouichi. "But it's indisputable that before that, he caused considerable harm to this nation, is it not? I believe that your willingness to work with someone like that is unacceptable for someone from the Ten Master Clans. Do the rest of you not agree with me?"

Maya's nonchalance came from her firm belief that this was the real problem.

"Yes," Gouki Ichijou said succinctly—

"It's as Ms. Yotsuba says," added Atsuko Mutsuzuka—

"Unfortunately, I agree," concurred Raizou Yatsushiro—

"Mr. Saegusa, I advised you against this at the time," noted Katsuto Juumonji—

"I'm sure you had your reasons, Mr. Saegusa, but..." Isami Itsuwa said—

"I find your actions indefensible," Gen Mitsuya stated—

"Mr. Saegusa, whatever your intentions, there are people we simply cannot cooperate with. This is a line that must not be crossed," Mai Futatsugi agreed—

—All in support of Maya.

Kouichi, still smiling, was cornered.

Gouki, Atsuko, Raizou, Katsuto, Isami, Gen, and Mai all looked to Makoto Kudou, whose stance was not yet clear.

But what Mai had said to Kouichi applied to Makoto as well. Though the circumstances had been different, Makoto had also colluded with Gongjin Zhou.

Makoto's predicament was interrupted by a knock at the door.

"I don't suppose you'd mind letting me in." From the other side of the supposedly soundproofed door came the voice of an old man that everyone around the table knew very well.

Katsuto, who was sitting closest to the door, stood and glanced at the others for confirmation. Some nodded, and none shook their heads.

Katsuto walked over to the door and opened it.

On the other side was the ostensibly retired Retsu Kudou.

"It has been quite some time, master. It's good to see you. But what brings you here today?" Mai greeted him politely. Katsuto offered him his seat, but Retsu waved him off with a smile.

"You'll have to excuse me. I couldn't help but overhear the conversation just now," said Retsu, getting to the point immediately.

No one bothered asking how. The proceedings of the Master

Clans Council were supposed to be confidential, but it wasn't only the Kudou family who had ways of learning exactly what went on at the meeting.

"It's understandable that you all would condemn Kouichi. However, I'd like you to wait before assigning him the blame."

By using Kouichi's first name instead of calling him *Mr. Saegusa*, Retsu made it clear that he was speaking not as a former member of the Master Clans Council, but rather as a simple elder of Japan's magical community, and that his statement carried no authority but was merely the words of an elder.

"As far as abetting anti-magician activities, Kouichi consulted me about this. And I did not stop him."

Around the table, the council members looked to one another in confusion. Gouki, Mai, Gen, Isami, Atsuko, Raizou, and Katsuto—everyone except for Maya, Kouichi, and Makoto. None of them could guess what Retsu's intention was. No—Makoto, too, was baffled as to what his father could possibly mean. Only Maya and Kouichi had guessed Retsu's mind.

"Furthermore, the Kudou family likewise had a relationship with Gongjin Zhou. Kouichi colluded with him, but they merely traded information—they didn't take any concrete action. But Gongjin Zhou provided me with the magical technology behind parasite-powered unmanned magic weapons, and using those techniques, I made innocent young people into experimental subjects. If Maya's son hadn't stopped me, the consequences could have been terrible."

The council's gazes shifted from Retsu to Maya, who smiled faintly. She had planned an all-out attack on Kouichi, but that didn't mean she wasn't open to changing that plan. If Retsu was going to cover for Kouichi, she had no intention of ruining their master-disciple moment.

"Compared to what I did, Kouichi's actions were merely play-acting at intrigue."

"But, master—," Gouki began, but Retsu silenced him with a look.

"The Kudou family will surrender its seat on the Ten Master Clans. Would that satisfy this council?"

"Sir…" Makoto looked up at his father's face, stunned.

Retsu's name meant *fierce*, and his gaze lived up to that name as he looked toward his son. "Makoto, you are guilty of personally harboring Gongjin Zhou. The incident involving the Taoists he dispatched caused serious trouble for both Ms. Yotsuba's son and Mr. Ichijou's son. In truth, this is something you should be saying, not me."

"Sir…Father!"

"Makoto, I'm disappointed in you."

It was Maya who spoke up to placate Retsu. "If you are saying that the Kudou family will take full responsibility, then the Yotsuba family will accept that. So long as Mr. Saegusa is willing to make reparations for his misconduct with his future contributions, I am content."

Retsu was not only covering for Kouichi because of his feelings for his student. If feelings had come into play at all, then it was because Makoto was his son.

Currently, the most powerful group of magicians in Japan was not the military's magician unit but rather the Yotsuba family—and the Saegusa family. They were the two crown jewels of Japanese magic society. It would be disruptive for the Saegusa family to be expelled from the Ten Master Clans. It was necessary to keep them there, in order to preserve the balance of the families that stood at the pinnacle of Japanese magic.

In order to protect the stability of the Ten Master Clans he himself had created, Retsu Kudou had covered for Kouichi Saegusa. It wasn't hard for Maya to understand why he would do something like that.

"If you say so, Ms. Yotsuba…"

"It's true that the void left by the absence of the Saegusa family would be too large," said Atsuko and Raizou in succession, agreeing with Maya—but her glance at Kouichi was just as cold as ever.

There were no other dissenting voices.

Kouichi simply watched on, his face an unsmiling mask.

"Come, Makoto. We're leaving."

Thus ordered by Retsu, Makoto unsteadily vacated his seat at the table of the Ten Master Clans.

"If you'll excuse us," said Retsu lightly to the room, then exited.

Makoto followed behind him, shoulders slumping.

The door closed with a *thunk*.

"W-well, then," Isami Itsuwa began, his slightly nervous voice seemingly restarting the flow of time. "We will need to decide which family will be replacing the Kudou family."

"The selection conference is tomorrow. Would that not be a better time?" objected Gen Mitsuya.

"When there's a vacancy in the Ten Master Clans, the Clans are to choose an interim member to fulfill the position's duties until the next selection conference can formally choose a replacement. The Ten Master Clans cannot remain incomplete for even a day," Mai Futatsugi piped up without missing a beat. With Makoto gone, she was now the oldest member present.

"You're right. Who shall we choose? Does anyone have any candidates to suggest?" Gouki said, looking resigned.

"Well," began Maya, instantly commanding the attention of the others. "How about Mr. Shippou? Takumi, the family head, is a judicious man, and although he has relatively few magicians below him, he commands considerable financial resources."

Gouki, Katsuto, and Isami all looked to Kouichi. The antagonism between the Saegusa family and the Shippou family was well-known, but Kouichi showed no reaction to Maya's suggestion.

"Mr. Shippou, you say? ...Are there any other nominations?" Mai asked.

The assembled family heads offered no answer to the question.

"Very well, then. It's decided—the newest member of the Ten Master Clans is Mr. Shippou. It may only be for a single day, but we should inform him immediately."

"I'll go," Katsuto said, raising his hand, and stood to leave the room in order to make the necessary phone call.

"Mr. Juumonji, please wait a moment," Mai said to Katsuto, whose back was already turned. "Let's take a short recess. Shall we reconvene in thirty minutes?"

There were no objections.

The next day was Tuesday, February 5.

Immediately after arriving in the Class 2-E classroom, Tatsuya was paid a visit by Takuma Shippou.

But before Tatsuya could even reply, Takuma's senior on the club management committee, Tomitsuka, spoke up curiously. "Hey, Shippou. What's going on?"

"Ah, I just wanted to, er, thank Shiba…" replied Takuma awkwardly.

And his awkwardness was quite understandable. The fuss that Takuma had caused the previous April with his series of duels was well-known throughout the school.

Takuma had subsequently tried to reform himself, a fact both his freshman classmates and upperclassmen were well aware of, but that didn't erase the memory of his terrible rudeness to Tatsuya from their minds. Takuma coming to see Tatsuya at all, whatever the reason, was sufficient cause for a number of curious gazes.

Added to those were Erika and Leo's sharp, nasty glances. Mikihiko was also in Class 2-E today, and his expression was just as displeased as theirs.

"Thank me? I can't imagine what for."

Takuma's rescue came in the form of Tatsuya's utter lack of grudge. Far from it—Tatsuya had seen Takuma's efforts during the Nine School Competition and regarded the way he'd dusted himself off and got back up quite highly.

"Er...I heard that Ms. Yotsuba recommended my family as the interim member of the Master Clans Council, so..."

"Sorry, this is the first I've heard of it." It was true; he wasn't feigning ignorance. The fact that there was an interim member of the Ten Master Clans meant that one of the previous members had left. Tatsuya found it difficult to guess at what sort of major incident might have caused such a thing.

"I mean...it's an interim position so it will only last until today... but still, I'm really happy about it. So thank you!"

His business concluded, an embarrassed-looking Takuma fled to the safety of his own classroom.

Tatsuya considered the various reasons why Takuma would be fixated on his family's position among the Ten Master Clans. Was it really something to be so happy about?

Different people really did have different ways of seeing the world, Tatsuya realized anew.

It was the day of the Ten Master Clans Selection Conference, an event which took place but once every four years. The heads of the Eighteen Support Clans were all in attendance, surrounding the table at which the Ten Master Clans sat. Only the Kudou family was absent.

"I call to order the Ten Master Clans Selection Conference."

At Mai Futatsugi's declaration, all present stood.

"First, as is custom, those with objections to the current membership of the Ten Master Clans please remain standing. Those without objections, please sit within the next minute."

This was the first stage of the selection conference's voting process.

If even a single person remained standing, paper ballots would be distributed, and a signed vote would be taken. Each vote contained the ten families the voter considered most suitable to be on the Ten Master Clans. The votes would be counted immediately under the supervision of three members from the Ten Master Clans and three members of the Eighteen Support Clans, and the results would determine the new composition of the Ten Master Clans.

Significantly, the ballots were signed. The Ten Master Clans were meant to be comprised of the most powerful of the Twenty-Eight Families in a given moment. However, the criteria for what constituted *powerful* was not merely a family's magical prowess but also their ability to contribute to the nation as a whole.

Voting for an unsuitable family would not—as it had once in the old days—result in a family being stripped of its number. Still, the penalty of being seen as a poor judge of quality for the next four years was heavy enough.

The first to take their seat at Mai's words were the ten people at the roundtable.

Then, one after another, the eighteen family heads around them began to sit down.

When the clock's second hand had traveled 180 degrees from where it had been, a surprising thing happened.

The heads of the Kuki and Kuzumi families both took their seats.

They had both been expected to recommend the Kudou family, which had been dismissed the previous day, so this move was a shock to those family heads among the Eighteen Support Clans who had been planning for a vote to be held.

The family heads who remained standing exchanged glances.

Then, by ones and twos, they began to sit, like so many teeth falling out. By the time fifty seconds had passed, no one was left standing.

When the second hand completed its revolution, Mai Futatsugi stood again. "Very well. For the next four years, the Ichijou, Futatsugi, Miyaki, Yotsuba, Itsuwa, Mutsuzuka, Saegusa, Shippou, Yatsushiro, and Juumonji families will serve as the Ten Master Clans. We ask you all for your continuing support."

The nine others at the roundtable stood and, along with Mai, turned around and bowed.

A round of applause for the new Ten Master Clans arose from the heads of the Eighteen Support clans.

Normally, once the selection of the Ten Master Clans was complete, the heads of the Eighteen Support Clans would be dismissed, leaving the Ten to commence discussion of their new structure. However, as they made to leave, Mai addressed the Kuki and Kuzumi family heads. "Ms. Kuki, Mr. Kuzumi, remain for a moment, please."

"Ms. Futatsugi?"

"Is something the matter?"

"I have a favor to ask the two of you, if you'll give me just a moment of your time."

The Kuki and Kuzumi family heads both nodded. Once the other heads of the Eighteen had left, the people remaining in the room were the Ten Master Clan heads and the two who'd been asked to stay— both of whom hailed from families associated with the number nine.

"What I'd like to ask you is this—"

"Ms. Futatsugi, if I may." It was Takumi Shippou, the head of the family who'd only barely joined the Ten Master Clans, who spoke. "Ms. Kuki, Mr. Kuzumi— My family, the Shippou family, has been honored with a seat on the Ten Master Clans, but we are, to be blunt— We are insufficient. Properly speaking, we ought to move our residence and begin oversight of the Kyoto region in place of the Kudou family. However, that is far beyond what my family is capable of."

"In that case, perhaps you should ask Ms. Futatsugi and Ms. Yotsuba for assistance? And if Kyoto is the problem, then I believe it overlaps with part of Mr. Ichijou's area of responsibility."

Takumi smiled and shook his head at the suggestion from the

woman who was the head of the Kuki family. "That is one option, but for my part I would prefer that the Kudou family continue to watch over the Kyoto-Shiga area and Kii Peninsula. Of course, the Shippou family will not be so uncouth as to only ask favors of other families. Might I offer my family's insufficient power to you, the families of Nine?"

"Understood."

"Once we've consulted with Makoto, I'm certain that we will bring you a favorable answer."

"I am in your debt." Takumi bowed deeply, and not to be out-done, the heads of the Kuki and Kuzumi families did likewise.

The Kuki and Kuzumi family heads were dismissed, and the mood in the meeting room became slightly more relaxed.

"Now then, shall we resume the Master Clans Council?" said Mai.

"There are the measures in response to the humanists to consider, yes," Gen answered.

Gouki preempted the topic. "No, before that, I'd like to hear about the suspicious vessel off the coast of Izu."

"Mr. Ichijou…that's an extremely recent development," Isami said, looking exasperated.

"If it's a terrorist ship, they're not going to wait around for us." Gouki was undeterred.

"I don't mind, Mr. Itsuwa," Kouichi said, having regained his usual demeanor after a night's sleep.

"Let's hear it, then." Kouichi may have been his old self, but Gouki had no intention of dealing with him as though nothing had happened. For Gouki, collusion with an enemy of the state was not something to be forgiven easily.

"There was no sign of a magician aboard the freighter that Ms. Yotsuba identified for us. No traces of weapons or ammunition within the vessel, either."

"And by that, you mean—?"

"There's a possibility that the explosives were transported else-where. The vessel in question may also have been obtained as an escape route, so we plan to continue observing it."

"And what about the USNA's movements?" It was Katsuto, rather than Gouki, who posed this question to Kouichi.

"We've found some of their field agents—fellows who turned and now work for the USNA—but their tradecraft is not particularly impressive. It's hard to imagine this is an official operation."

"So…their real hunter must be hiding somewhere."

"We've confirmed that the yacht Ms. Yotsuba told us about is outside of our territorial waters. Surprisingly, he may be hiding there."

Isami wore a thoughtful expression at Kouichi's answer.

"If they're in the open water, shall I go poke them? If we disguise it as a natural disaster, we should be able to deny involvement."

"Surely the problem is the terrorist who may have already entered the country, not this USNA hunter," said Atsuko, taking the opposite side of Isami's position.

"That is true. While there's no proof he's here, there's also no proof he isn't. Not knowing where he might be lurking is the worst possible position to be in," said Raizou, supporting Atsuko's point. "He could even be targeting the Master Clans Council, for all we know."

It was surely a pure coincidence.

But in fact—

The moment after Raizou spoke those words, the meeting room was assaulted by a tremendous noise.

Tuesday, February 5, 2097, 10:33 AM

At First High, students were milling about during the break between first and second periods.

Tatsuya checked a message on his personal terminal, and uncharacteristically, the color drained from his face.

"Sorry, I gotta go!"

Leaving behind Mizuki and the other classmates he'd been walking with, he sprinted toward the practice room.

Having gotten permission from Jennifer Smith, the school guidance counselor, Tatsuya was excused from school. As he came out onto the broad tree-lined path that led to the front gate, he encountered Miyuki.

"Did you get an urgent message, too, Tatsuya?" Miyuki asked quickly, her face totally pale.

"Let's hurry," Tatsuya assented, wasting even fewer words.

Miyuki nodded and quickened her stride, but a voice from behind her stopped her short.

The Course 1 students who emerged from the exit were Minami, her classmate Kasumi Saegusa, Kasumi's younger sister Izumi, and Takuma Shippou. All had ties to the Ten Master Clans. And aside from Minami, all were related to their family heads by blood.

"Miyuki!" Izumi came running up to Miyuki.

"You got a message, too, Izumi?"

"It's not a false alarm, is it?!"

Miyuki shook her head.

Izumi started to tremble.

"We're going to see what happened. What about you guys?" asked Tatsuya from a step back.

"I'm coming, too!" Takuma declared immediately.

"Yeah, us too!" Kasumi announced, taking her sister's trembling hand.

Minami came alongside Miyuki, ready to raise her shield at a moment's notice.

With Tatsuya in the lead, the six students set off for the station.

Meanwhile, at Third High—

"Masaki, what happened?!" Kichijouji demanded, his breath ragged after chasing after Masaki, who'd rushed out of their classroom to the faculty office to be excused from school.

"My father's been in an attack!" Masaki answered over his shoulder, reluctant to slow down for even a moment.

"An attack?! Isn't he at the Master Clans Council right now...?"

"Yeah, and the Master Clans Council site just got hit by a suicide bomber!"

"What?!"

Masaki finally looked back at his speechless friend. "The emergency message alone doesn't tell us anything. All we know is that they're still alive. I'm gonna take a chopper to the site of the attack. I'm leaving Akane and the others to you, George!"

"R-right, okay! Take care, Masaki!"

"I know, I will!"

Masaki sprinted away, heading not for his home but for the helipad at his family's company's office building.

Meanwhile, at the Magic University—

Mayumi bolted to her feet in the middle of a classroom.

"Saegusa, what's the matter?" asked the startled woman teaching the discussion class.

"I'm very sorry, ma'am—could I talk to you for a second?" Mayumi had an awkward, embarrassed expression on her face as she walked toward the instructor as quickly as she could without seeming frantic. She discreetly showed her personal terminal's screen to the instructor.

The instructor was about to exclaim in surprise, but Saegusa stifled her with a gesture, then leaned to whisper in her ear. "I'm sure my family members at home are feeling anxious. Since I'm sure my brother is on his way to the scene, I'd like to head home and help everyone calm down."

The instructor nodded, her expression serious.

Mayumi smiled pleasantly to keep the other students from suspecting anything, then apologetically explained that she had to leave because of a family emergency.

The explosion had happened right outside the conference room. The doors were blown in, and crimson flames licked at the walls.

But the fire was soon extinguished.

"Excellent work, Mr. Juumonji."

Not a single member of the Master Clans Council had sustained so much as a scratch. Both heat and explosive force had been perfectly deflected by Katsuto's heat-resistant shield.

"You're no slouch yourself, Ms. Mutsuzuka."

The fire had been snuffed out by Atsuko Mutsuzuka's heat control. For magicians in the heat-controlling "Six" families, putting out a fire that couldn't even melt steel beams was a walk in the park.

"We should get outside. If we let ourselves get buried, it'll be that much harder to escape," Mai Futatsugi suggested calmly as she delayed further oxidation of the building's materials, in order to prevent the spread of fire and the release of toxic gasses.

"I agree. This appears to be a rather large-scale terrorist bombing," said Gen Mitsuya with a nod, holding several magic programs at the ready.

"Puppet terrorism! This is an atrocity," Gouki spat. *Puppet terrorism* was the term for using human puppets as a delivery method for suicide bombs. The psychological manipulation required to turn a human into a puppet could be done via magic or pharmaceutical means, and there were ways of robbing someone's control of their body via magic.

The Ichijou and other "One" families specialized in biological interference magic, but magically controlling other human's physical movements was forbidden. Some families had had their numbers stripped and become Extras for this very crime. For that reason, even though he intimately understood the process of puppet terrorism, Gouki had no way of interfering with the control method and stopping it.

"Damn!" Realizing that the floor was about to collapse, Raizou Yatsushiro activated his gravity control magic. Holding up a wide area of floor that had lost its supports so it was steady enough to walk on, Raizou made the usual flight magic seem trivial by comparison.

"We should hurry," said Kouichi. The rest nodded, and moving in a closely packed group with Maya, Mai, and Atsuko in the center, they started to find their way out of the hotel.

Facing the human bombs wandering around in the hallway, Gouki Ichijou used Burst. "This isn't a suicide bombing. They're using reanimated corpses to carry the bombs!" Gouki growled as he blasted the arms off the bodies to prevent them from detonating their explosives. The attack method was even more despicable than he'd realized.

In order to avoid being buried by the collapsing floors, the heads of the Ten Master Clans had decided to escape by jumping from the roof, so upward they headed, dispatching the bombers as they went.

Gen Mitsuya and Kouichi Saegusa were the fastest at dealing with the corpse bombs. Gen had a technique called Speed Loader, which allowed him to store up to nine programs and release them all simultaneously, while Kouichi's Octet allowed him to hold eight types of magic from four systems, each program ready at the moment before its activation, then freely choose which to activate based on what the situation demanded. The walking corpses had no chance.

Meanwhile, Katsuto's Phalanx, a broad-spectrum defense magic, provided perfect protection against the odd corpse bomb that slipped through.

Raizou's gravity control magic was kept busy managing the collapsing building and preventing its complete structural failure.

Fire extinguishing was handled by Atsuko's heat control.

Mai Futatsugi dispersed toxic gas and fumes.

With the fires out, the halls were dark, and Maya provided light as no flashlights were available.

Isami Itsuwa and Takumi Shippou had absolutely nothing to do.

It was impossible for any terrorist attack using explosives a human could pick up and carry to kill or wound the members of this group. The family heads had long since realized this.

"The media spin for this is going to be a major pain," grumbled Gen as he riddled another corpse with holes.

"I can't imagine there'll be a way to cover something like this up, will there?" Atsuko said, exasperated, as she put out a wall of flame.

"I've gotten plenty of footage of the bomb-carrying corpses, but... it feels like releasing it publicly will have the opposite effect," Isami agreed. He had given up on his magic abilities being called upon and was instead capturing video footage.

"Maybe so, but I still think purposefully injuring ourselves is pointless," Maya stated.

Raizou's shoulders sagged. "I suppose we'll just have to stay hidden until the outrage dies out."

It wasn't clear whether Raizou was joking or being serious, but either way, no one spoke up to disagree.

Tuesday, February 5, 2097, 10:30 AM

The final count of fatalities from the catastrophic bombing of the hotel in Hakone was twenty-two, with thirty injured.

Meanwhile, thirty-three occupants of the hotel were uninjured. Of them, we've been told that twenty-seven were magicians.

There has been an outpouring of criticism toward the magicians, who are accused of focusing on their own safety in the immediate aftermath of the attack.

(○○○ Newspaper, electronic edition, February 6, 2097 issue)

AFTERWORD

I hope you all enjoyed *The Irregular at Magic High School, Volume 17: The Master Clans Council (Part I)*. There weren't a lot of action scenes this time, but to make up for that, I packed it chock-full of angsty emotions! (Just kidding.)

It's not necessarily the case that behind every successful couple is a trail of brokenhearted men and women. I actually think that it's more common for people to be happy for them, or if not that, at least take a *hey, get with whoever you want* attitude. And for the couple themselves, there's nothing better than the people around them celebrating their relationship.

However, it's not uncommon for heartbreak to lead to romantic relationships between friends, acquaintances, and even rivals. It happens in the real world, and it's even more common in fiction.

But what about encouraging parents to break up a couple? I wonder. Your humble author personally believes that's something you should only do before the couple is engaged. In the case of [SPOILER REDACTED], they obviously agree, for which the couple in question is probably grateful. Although it does feel like too little, too late.

But they must think of [SPOILER REDACTED] as being a

serious nuisance. This person's true intentions notwithstanding, of course.

This was Lina's first appearance in a year, although it ended up being a little different than the preview illustration suggested. She's a really easy character to write, so I'd like to have her show up more, but...at the moment, she's not allowed to leave America. So for a while, when she does show up, it's going to be like she did in this volume. Alas.

Now then, about the next volume, aka part 2 of the Master Clans Council arc. Like the Visitor arc, this one ended up being three parts long. Structurally, there are parts of it that are similar to the Visitor arc as well. Some of it might also be familiar from the *Irregular: Out of Order* and *Lost Zero* video games.

...I feel like if I say anything else, I'm going to get yelled at for spoiling things, so I hope you'll look forward to the next installment.

Tsutomu Sato